"Nanny Stowe is so looking forward to meeting you."

No more than he was, Beau thought darkly.

As he stepped into the majestic stairhall, his gaze automatically traveled up the flight of broad steps that gradually narrowed to the landing. A woman stood poised there, the light beaming in behind her seeming to set her hair aflame. This woman would have to be the most stunningly gorgeous, sexiest creature he'd ever seen in his life.

And she was *Nanny Stowe?*

A sharply unsettling question darted through the fog in Beau's brain.

What had his grandfather been doing with her?

Two years she'd been under this roof and his grandfather, according to Wallace, had definitely not fallen into his second childhood. The more Beau thought about the situation, it became disturbingly clear that Nanny Stowe was mistress of the house.

Dear Reader,

We hope you've been enjoying Harlequin Presents®' NANNY WANTED! series, in which some of our most popular authors have created nannies whose talents have extended way beyond taking care of children!

Emma Darcy's novel brings you a nanny with a difference. She's a woman of mystery—and incredible good looks—who is part of the household Beau Prescott inherits. Is she genuine in her reasons for being there, or is she the scheming woman he imagines? Read on as the startling truth is revealed.

Remember—nanny knows best when it comes to falling in love!

The Editors

Look out next month for:

THE NANNY AFFAIR by Robyn Donald (#1980)

EMMA DARCY

Inherited: One Nanny

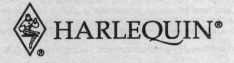

TORONTO • NEW YORK • LONDON
AMSTERDAM • PARIS • SYDNEY • HAMBURG
STOCKHOLM • ATHENS • TOKYO • MILAN • MADRID
PRAGUE • WARSAW • BUDAPEST • AUCKLAND

To Sue—for flaunting her fortieth birthday with
a brilliant party where my friends Dr. Nick Smith,
Dr. Geoffrey McCarthy and Dr. Harvey Adams happily
informed me of the etiquette in delivering the results of a
pregnancy test and insisted I acknowledge their
contribution to this story.

ISBN 0-373-11972-0

INHERITED: ONE NANNY

First North American Publication 1998.

Copyright © 1998 by Emma Darcy.

All rights reserved. Except for use in any review, the reproduction or
utilization of this work in whole or in part in any form by any electronic,
mechanical or other means, now known or hereafter invented, including
xerography, photocopying and recording, or in any information storage
or retrieval system, is forbidden without the written permission of the
publisher, Harlequin Enterprises Limited, 225 Duncan Mill Road,
Don Mills, Ontario, Canada M3B 3K9.

All characters in this book have no existence outside the imagination of
the author and have no relation whatsoever to anyone bearing the same
name or names. They are not even distantly inspired by any individual
known or unknown to the author, and all incidents are pure invention.

This edition published by arrangement with Harlequin Books S.A.

® and TM are trademarks of the publisher. Trademarks indicated with
® are registered in the United States Patent and Trademark Office, the
Canadian Trade Marks Office and in other countries.

Printed in U.S.A.

CHAPTER ONE

A NANNY?

The question had niggled Beau Prescott on and off throughout the fourteen hour flight from Buenos Aires to Sydney. It had reared its tantalising head from the very first reading of his grandfather's will, pertinently included with all the other official notices sent to him in the solicitor's packet. Now that his journey home was almost over and he was about to get answers, it pushed once more to the forefront of his mind.

Why on earth had his grandfather employed a nanny for the last two years of his life? And why was she listed in the will as another responsibility to be inherited by Beau, along with the rest of the family retainers?

A nanny made no sense to him. There weren't any children living in his grandfather's household. None he knew of anyway. Certainly none had been named in the will. There seemed absolutely no point in including a nanny—whoever she was—amongst the staff who were to remain as his dependents for at least another year, if not for the rest of their lives.

It was different with the others. Beau was completely in sympathy with looking after Mrs. Featherfield who was virtually an institution as his grandfather's housekeeper. Sedgewick, the butler, and Wallace, the chauffeur, had almost equal longevity. As for Mr. Polly, the head gardener, tipping him out of his beloved grounds was inconceivable. Each one of them deserved every consideration. But a nanny-come-lately without any children to mind?

Beau turned her name over in his mind...Margaret Stowe. Margaret sounded rather old-fashioned, spinsterish. For some reason he linked Stowe with stowaway. She could be a lame-dog nanny, fallen on hard times. His grandfather had a habit of taking in the occasional oddity, putting them on their feet again. But two years of largesse and an inclusion in the will seemed a bit much.

"We will be landing at Mascot on schedule," the pilot announced. "The weather is fine, current temperature nineteen degrees Celsius. Forecast for today is..."

Beau looked out his window and felt his stomach curl, hit by a wave of grief he'd been holding at bay since he'd received the news of his grandfather's death. The distinctive features of Sydney were spread out below, the predominance of red roofs, the harbour, the bridge, the opera house. This view had always meant coming home to him. But home had also meant Vivian Prescott, the man who'd taken in his orphaned eight-year-old grandson and given him the world as his playground.

Not so much of a grandfather as a grand person, Beau thought, keenly feeling the huge bite that had been taken so abruptly, so shockingly out of his life. Vivian Prescott had lived on a grand scale, had cultivated a grand approach to everything he'd done. His heart should have been grand enough to last a lot longer.

Vivian...now there was a name that would make

most men cringe. The Prescott family had a history of bestowing eccentric names. Beau had often winced over his, but his grandfather...never! He'd rejoiced in having one he considered uniquely his. "It means *life*, my boy. And *joie de vivre* is what I'm about."

He'd carried it with such panache, he'd made it perfectly acceptable, a natural extension of his highly individual personality, a positive expression of artistic flair and style, a provocative emphasis to the wickedly teasing twinkle in his ever-young eyes. It was almost impossible to believe he was actually gone and it hurt like hell not to have been there with him before he died.

A spurt of anger overlaid the grief. Damn it all! His grandfather had no business dying at eighty-six. He'd always boasted he'd live to a hundred, smoking his favourite cigars, drinking the best French champagne, a pretty woman hanging on each arm as he swanned through all the glittering charity events on his social calendar. He'd loved life too much to ever let go of it.

Beau heaved a sigh to relieve the tightness in his chest and told himself it was futile foolishness to feel cheated of more time with his grandfather. The fault was in his own complacency for letting almost three years go by without a visit home. It was all very well to excuse himself on the grounds of finding South America an explorer's paradise. A trip home now and then wouldn't have been a hardship. It simply had never occurred to him that the old man's long run of good health might be failing.

There'd been no hint of it in his letters. But then there'd been no mention of a nanny, either. Beau

frowned again over the vexing puzzle. If his grandfather had been sick, surely he would have hired a
nurse, not a nanny. Unless…no, he couldn't—
wouldn't—believe his grandfather had gone the least
bit senile. There had to be some other answer.

The plane landed. The moment it stopped, Beau
was out of his seat and opening the overhead locker
for his flight bag, wanting to be off with as little delay
as possible.

"May I help you, Mr. Prescott?"

It was the cute air hostess who'd been so eager and
willing to look after his every need on the trip. Beau
flashed her a smile. "No, I'm fine, thank you." She
was a honey but he wasn't interested in taking up the
invitation in her eyes. His mind was on serious business, no room for play.

Nevertheless, he was aware of her lustful once-over
as he moved past her to the exit tunnel and felt a slight
twinge of regret. He'd been womanless for a while,
busy mapping out a new trek up the Amazon. Still,
he'd never had a problem attracting a woman when
he was ready for one. Being over six feet tall and
having a body packed with muscles seemed to be a
turn-on to most of them, even when he looked scruffy
from being too long in uncivilised areas.

His mouth twitched as he remembered his grandfather calling it *his curse*. "It's too easy for you, my
boy, and if you keep taking the pickings, you'll never
know the fruits of settling down with a good
woman."

"I have no interest in settling down, Grandpa,"
he'd answered.

It was still true three years later, yet his grand-father's reply plucked at his conscience now.

"Beau, you're thirty years old. It's time you thought of having children. As it stands, you're the last of our family line, and I for one, don't like the thought of our gene pool coming to an end. It's our only claim to immortality, having a line that goes on after we die."

Had the old man been feeling his mortality then?

"Grandpa, there's no time limit on a man to have children," he'd argued. "Didn't Charlie Chaplin have them into his nineties? I bet you could still have one yourself."

"You need to stick around to bring them up right. Think about it, Beau. Your parents weren't much older than you are now when their plane crashed in Antarctica. No second chances for them. If you don't take time out from your travelling to get married and start a family, it may be too late before you know it."

Too late...misery dragged at Beau's heart. Too late to say goodbye to the wonderful old man who'd given him so much. Too late to say one last thank-you. Too late to even attend the funeral, held while Beau was still deep in the Amazon valley, out of range of any modern form of communication.

All he could do now was carry out his grandfather's will as it had been set out for him, even to keeping a useless nanny in his employ for another year. And making Rosecliff—the Prescott palace—his residence for the same period of time.

Maybe the latter was his grandfather's solution to making his footloose grandson stay still for a while, long enough to marry and start a family. Beau shook his head in wry dismissal of the idea. He wasn't ready for it. He felt no need for it. Making it happen would be wrong for everybody concerned. Scouting Europe was next on his agenda. He wasn't about to set that aside, and it was plain irresponsible to establish a nest he knew he'd be flying out of.

His long-legged stride beat all the other passengers to the immigration counter. He was through that bit of officialdom in no time and luckily his duffel bag was amongst the first pieces of luggage on the carousel. Having hefted it onto his back, and with nothing to declare, Beau headed straight for the arrival hall.

As he came down the ramp he spotted Wallace, his grandfather's chauffeur, smartly attired in the uniform he was so proud of—convinced it added a dignified stature to his shortness—and clearly determined on maintaining the correct standard of service.

The sense of emptiness that had been eating at Beau was suddenly flooded with warmth. Wallace had taught him everything he knew about cars. Wallace had acted as father-confessor through troubled times. Wallace was much more than a chauffeur. He was family and had been since Beau was eight years old.

"It is so good to see you, sir," Wallace greeted in heartfelt welcome, his eyes moistening.

Beau hugged him, moved by affection and a rush of protectiveness, patting him on the back as though the wiry little man was now the child in need of comfort. He had to be feeling the loss of Vivian Prescott as much, if not more than Beau. Wallace was in his late fifties and though spry for his age and certainly competent at his job, probably too old to start over with a new employer. His future was undoubtedly feeling very uncertain. Beau silently vowed to fix that, one way or another.

"I'm sorry I wasn't here, Wallace," he said, drawing back to re-establish appropriate dignity.

"Nothing you could have done for him, sir," came the quick assurance. "No warning. He just went in his sleep, like he always said he wanted to, right after a bang-up party. As Nanny Stowe says, the Angel of Death took him kindly."

The unctious Angel of Death declaration instantly conjured up a complacently righteous woman stuffed full of sweet homilies. Beau barely stopped himself from rolling his eyes. He had to bite his tongue, as well. Nanny Stowe clearly had Wallace's respect. Giving voice to a stomach-felt, "Yuk!" was definitely out of place.

He managed a smile. "Well, a bang-up party was certainly Grandpa's style."

"That it was, sir. Always had marvellous parties."

Beau's smile turned into a rueful grimace. "I should have at least been here to organise a fitting funeral for him."

"Not to worry, sir. Nanny Stowe took care of it."

"Did she now?"

Beau balefully added officious busybody to complacent and sickeningly righteous. How dare a mere nanny take over his grandfather's funeral? Sedgewick would have known what was required, having butlered for Vivian Prescott for nigh on thirty years, but a nanny who hadn't rated highly enough to be mentioned by his grandfather while he was alive? Beau was deeply offended at the high-handedness of the woman. Who the hell did she think she was?

"Well, let's get on home. The sooner the better," he said, feeling distinctly eager to let Nanny Stowe know her presumptuous reign of authority was over.

"Can I take your bags, sir?"

"This one." He handed over the flight bag for Wallace to feel useful. "Might as well leave the other on my back." The little man's knees would probably buckle under the weight of it.

"I could get a luggage trolley, sir."

"Waste of time." He waved towards the exit doors and set off, steering Wallace into accompanying him through the crowd of people still waiting for other arrivals. "I'd like you to tell me about the funeral," he added through gritted teeth, wanting to know the worst before he met the interloping nanny.

The chauffeur looked pleased to oblige. "We did him proud, sir. As Nanny Stowe said, it had to be a grand funeral for a grand man. And so it was, sir."

"How grand, Wallace?' Beau demanded, extremely dubious that Nanny Stowe would have a full appreciation of his grandfather's scale of grandness.

"Well, sir, we started with a splendid service in St. Andrew's Cathedral. It was packed. People overflowing outside and on the streets. Couldn't fit everyone in. Nanny Stowe got the notification list together and it included all the charity boards your grandfather sat on, all his friends from far and wide, politicians, everyone from the arts. It was a big, big turn-up."

At least she got that much right, Beau brooded.

"You know how your grandfather loved handing out red roses..."

His trademark.

"You've never seen as many red roses as there

were in that cathedral. I reckon Nanny Stowe must have cornered the market on them. They covered the casket, too. And everyone who came to the service was handed a red rose in remembrance.''

A nice touch, Beau grudgingly conceded.

They emerged from the hall into bright morning sunshine. A sparkling blue-sky day, Beau thought, his spirits lifting slightly. The chauffeur pointed to where the car was parked and they turned in that direction.

"Go on, Wallace," Beau urged. "Describe the service to me."

"Well, sir, the boys' choir sang beautifully. They started off with 'Prepare ye the way for The Lord' from the musical, *Godspell*. It was one of his favourites, as you know. Loved the theatre, your grandfather did."

"Yes. It gave him a lot of pleasure," Beau agreed, beginning to have a bit more respect for Nanny Stowe. The woman did have some creative thought, though it probably stemmed from an ingrained attention to detail. A nitpicking fusspot came to mind, nothing escaping her eye or ear. Nevertheless, his grandfather would have relished the theatrical note at his funeral service so however it came about could not be overly criticised.

"Sir Roland from the Arts Council made a wonderful speech…"

His grandfather's closest friend. The obvious choice.

"The bishop got a bit heavy with his words, I thought, but the readings from the bible were just right. Nanny Stowe chose them. All about generosity of spirit."

''Mmmh...' Beau wondered if Nanny Stowe was plotting to spark generosity of spirit in him, too.

The Rolls-Royce was parked, as usual, in a No Parking zone. Beau reminded himself to ask Wallace how he got away with that, but he had other things on his mind right now.

''The choir finished with a very stirring 'Amazing Grace.' Beautiful, it was,'' Wallace went on, as he opened the trunk of the car to load in Beau's luggage. ''Then at the graveside, we had a lone piper playing tunes of glory. Sedgewick thought of that. Your grandfather was very partial to a pipe band when he was in his cups, if you'll pardon the expression, sir.''

''Good for Sedgewick.'' Beau warmly approved. Nanny Stowe hadn't known everything! She'd probably be the type to follow the ''early to bed, early to rise'' maxim and had never witnessed his grandfather in his cups.

''What about the wake?'' he asked, freeing himself of the duffel bag.

''Oh, we all knew what your grandfather would want there, sir. Oceans of French champagne, caviar, smoked salmon, pickled quails' eggs...everything he liked best. Mrs. Featherfield and Sedgewick made the list and Nanny Stowe got it all in. She said the cost was not to be a consideration. I hope that was right, sir.''

''Quite right, Wallace.''

Though he'd certainly be checking the accounts. A blithe disregard for expenses was fine for his grandfather. For such an attitude to be adopted by the ubiquitous Nanny Stowe raised a few ugly suspicions about where the money went. Feathering her own nest before the grandson and heir arrived might be right down her stowaway alley.

As he dumped the duffel bag in the trunk, Beau was wondering if the family solicitor had been holding a watching brief on his grandfather's estate while all this had been going on. Surely his legal responsibility didn't begin and end with posting off a set of official documents to Buenos Aires.

Beau was champing at the bit by the time Wallace had ushered him into the back seat of the Roller. Home first to scout the nanny situation, then straight off to check the legal position. However, there was one burning question that couldn't wait. As soon the car was in motion, he asked it.

"Why did my grandfather acquire a nanny, Wallace?"

"Well, you know how he liked to have his little jokes, sir. He said he needed to have a nanny on hand, ready to look after him when he slid into his second childhood since there was no telling when it might happen at his age."

That seemed to be taking provident care a bit far. "Was there any sign of encroaching second childhood, Wallace? Please be frank with me."

"Not at all, sir. Mr. Prescott was the same as he ever was, right up until the night he…um…passed over."

At least he was saved the Angel of Death this time. "But he kept the nanny on regardless," Beau probed for more information.

"Yes, sir. Said she was better for him than a gin and tonic."

Beau frowned. "She didn't stop him drinking, did she?"

"Oh, she wouldn't have dreamed of doing that, sir." Wallace sounded quite shocked at the idea. "Nanny Stowe is very sociable. Very sociable."

And knew which side of her bread was buttered, Beau thought darkly, making sure she kept in good with everyone. There seemed no point in further questioning. Nanny Stowe had Wallace sucked right in. He wasn't about to say a bad word about the woman, despite her staying on so long without any nanny duties to perform. Such dalliance smacked of very dubious integrity to Beau. He was glad the chance to make his own judgment on her was fast approaching.

"Do you mind if I use the car phone to call Sedgewick, sir? He particularly asked to let him know when we were on our way."

Beau couldn't resist one dry remark. "I'm surprised it isn't Nanny Stowe who wants to know."

"Sedgewick will inform her, sir."

Of course. "Go right ahead, Wallace. I wouldn't deprive anyone of the chance to put out the welcome mat for me."

And he hoped Nanny Stowe would be standing right in the middle of it, shaking in her boots!

CHAPTER TWO

FEELING extremely nervous about meeting Beau Prescott, Maggie once more studied the photograph Vivian had insisted she keep.

"That's my boy, Beau. *The wild child.*"

Her mouth curved whimsically at the epithet given to his grandson. The photograph was three years old, taken at Vivian's eighty-second birthday party, and the handsome hunk filling out a formal dinner suit in devastating style could hardly be called a child. Though there was an air of boyish recklessness in his grin, and a wild devil dancing in his eyes.

Green eyes. They were certainly very attractive set in a deeply tanned face and framed with streaky blond hair so thick it hadn't been fully tamed for the formality of the photograph. Nevertheless, its somewhat shaggy state was rather endearing, softening the hard, ruggedness of a strong-boned face and a squarish jaw. He had a nice mouth, the lips well-defined, neither too full nor too thin. He looked good, no doubt about it, but looks weren't everything.

"Tame him long enough to get him to the marriage altar and father a child with you, and Rosecliff and all that goes with it will be yours, Maggie."

How many times had Vivian put that proposition to her in the past two years? A challenging piece of mischief, Maggie had always thought, a running bit of fun between them. She'd never taken it seriously, usually making a joke of it—

"What would I want with him? You've spoilt me for younger men, Vivian. None of them have your *savoire faire* or charisma."

—or shrugging it off—

"I might not like him, Vivian. And there's no way I'd marry a man without at least liking him."

"Every woman likes Beau," was his stock answer.

"Well, he might not like me," she'd argued.

"What's not to like?"

Maggie had always let the banter slide at that point. Putting herself down in any shape or form was against her principles. She had a long history of a lot of mean people wanting to squash self-esteem out of her, treating her as worthless and of no account in the world, and she had determinedly risen above it. Nevertheless, too many disappointments had taught her liking could not be counted upon.

It had been one of the miracles of coming to this marvellous place, everyone on the staff liking her, welcoming her into the family, so to speak, and not a mean bone in any of them. Vivian had said she was his nanny and despite his highly eccentric notion of her job with him, she'd been accepted into the household as Nanny Stowe as though it were a perfectly normal position.

Vivian's oft-repeated idea of her roping in the wild child to extend the family line and ensure a succession of Prescotts at Rosecliff also met with general approval.

It was, of course, a totally mad idea.

Except it wasn't quite so mad anymore.

It was beginning to feel very much like a burden of responsibility.

Maggie shook her head, hopelessly uncomfortable with the pressure to perform. Yet it was there, and she couldn't shrug it off. Nor could she bring herself to snuff out the hope that was riding on her shoulders. People she cared about were hurting. And there was also the sense of not letting Vivian down.

"You weren't here. You have no idea how it is," she said accusingly to the photograph. "You shouldn't have been off in the wilds, Beau Prescott."

They'd had to handle it all without him. After the first couple of grief-stricken days following Vivian's untimely death, everyone had been so busy trying to get the funeral right, none of them had looked beyond it. Only when the funeral was over, did the loss really hit, and then the solicitor had come to spell out where they stood.

The one-year residency clause in the will had brought home the fact that Vivian Prescott was gone—really gone—and Rosecliff now belonged to his grandson who clearly had no use for it since he was always off travelling. After the stipulated year, the property could be sold or disposed of as he saw fit. Vivian Prescott's reign here was over, and so were their lives with him.

Maggie knew she could always fall on her feet somewhere else. At twenty-eight she was young enough to cope with a downturn in fortune and she'd had plenty of practice at making do with odd jobs in the years before meeting Vivian Prescott. Flexibility was her strong point. Though it would be hard leaving this magical mansion and its magnificent setting.

Harder still leaving the people who had given her the sense of being part of a real family.

However, it was like the end of their world for Mrs. Featherfield, and Sedgewick and Wallace and Mr. Polly. As young at heart as they all were, they would be viewed by other employers as at retirement age. If Beau Prescott decided to sell Rosecliff, where would they go? What would they do? Who would have them?

This was home to them. They didn't want to be split up. They didn't want to be dumped on the useless scrapheap, surviving on pensions. They weren't old. They had at least another twenty good years in them. Probably more.

The flurry of fear added a further weight of grief.

Then Sedgewick had remembered.

He'd stood up, elegantly tall and splendidly dignified, his ingrained authority providing a point of calm in the storm. His big, soulful brown eyes had fastened on Maggie, and there was not the slightest bit of tremulous doubt in his delivered opinion.

"Nanny Stowe, you can save us. Mr. Vivian wanted you to."

She'd shaken her head sadly. "I'm terribly sorry, Sedgewick. I simply don't have the power to change his will."

"You promised him...I heard you...the very night Mr. Vivian died. It was just before the guests arrived for the party and he asked me to pour you both a glass of champagne, remember?"

"Yes. But we were only chatting..."

"No. He said—I distinctly remember it—*Promise me you'll give it a chance with Beau when he comes home*. And you did. You clicked glasses with him and gave your promise.''

''It was only funning, Sedgewick.''

''Oh no! No, no, no, no!'' Mrs. Featherfield had clucked. ''Mr. Vivian was very serious about getting Master Beau married off to you, Nanny Stowe. He talked about it many, many times...to all of us,'' she'd added significantly.

''Always treated you like one of the family,'' Wallace had chimed in. ''That's where his sights were set. Getting it legal.''

Mr. Polly, his glorious gardens under threat of being taken over by someone else—or worse, destroyed by some developer—had stirred himself to put in his sage opinion. ''Matter of cross-pollination, getting the two of you together.''

''And in the light of Mr. Vivian's passing over that night,'' Sedgewick had added portentously, ''I think everyone must agree you gave him a deathbed promise, Nanny Stowe. One cannot disregard the gravity of a deathbed promise.''

''A chance, Sedgewick,'' Maggie had hastily pleaded. ''I only promised to give it a chance. There's no guarantee that Beau Prescott would ever see me as...as a desirable wife. Or, indeed, that I'd see him as a desirable husband.''

''But you'll give it a *good* chance, won't you, dear?' Mrs. Featherfield had pressed. ''And you do have a year to make the best of it.''

''Be assured you will have our every assistance,'' Sedgewick had declared.

''Hear, hear!'' they had all agreed, their eyes pinning Maggie down with their anxious hope.

She had wanted to say again and again it was only a joke, but to Sedgewick and Mrs. Featherfield and Wallace and Mr. Polly, it was deadly serious. Their future was at stake. Making some other life was unthinkable, and their expectations of continuing the status quo into the sunset were riding on her and what Mr. Vivian had wanted.

The truly dreadful part was they had convinced themselves she could bring it off—marry the heir, have his child, and they would all live happily ever after at Rosecliff. The doubts she voiced were brushed aside. Worse...they attacked the doubts by plotting outrageous ways to get around them. The goal was now fixed in their minds and it was so blindingly wonderful, they didn't want to see anything else.

Giving it a chance did not promise a certain result, she had warned each one of them.

And what were their replies?

Sedgewick, bending his head in soulful chiding, "Nanny Stowe, you know what Mr. Vivian always preached. *You must cultivate a positive attitude.*"

Attitude did not necessarily produce miracles!

Mrs. Featherfield, doing her endearing mother hen thing, "Think of a baby. A new baby at Rosecliff. I can't imagine anything more perfect."

Babies were not high on Maggie's agenda. She was only twenty-eight, not thirty-eight!

Wallace, a lecherous twinkle in his eye as he pointedly looked at the long tumbling mass of her red-gold hair. "No need to worry, Nanny Stowe. I can assure you Master Beau will take one look at you and his brain will register—*red hot mamma*. It'll be a piece of cake."

Maggie was not interested in the brain below Beau Prescott's belt! Not unless there was an engaging brain above it, as well.

Mr. Polly, tending his prize roses. "Nature will take its course, Nanny Stowe. A little help and care and you can always get the result you want."

Marriage, unfortunately, was not a bed of roses. It was a lot more complicated.

Maggie couldn't truthfully claim she absolutely didn't want it. Not having met the man, how could she know one way or the other? Even looking at Beau Prescott's photograph and assessing his physical attractions, she couldn't help feeling terribly uneasy with the situation.

It was fine for Vivian and all the faithful staff to dismiss the possibility of Beau Prescott's not liking her or her not liking him. They didn't *want* to admit the possibility. Maggie, however, had her reservations and many of them.

Besides, when it came to marriage, there was a matter of chemistry, too. Good-looking men had often left Maggie quite cold in the past. They were so full of themselves, there was no room for a two-way relationship. Not really. All they wanted was for a woman to fall on her back for them. Well, no thanks.

But maybe there could be magic with Beau Prescott. He did look very engaging in the photograph. If enough of Vivian had rubbed off on his grandson…

The ache in her heart intensified. Vivian Prescott had given her the most wonderful two years of her life. She hadn't realised quite how much she'd loved

that old man until...suddenly he wasn't here anymore...and never would be again.

Joie de vivre.

Did his grandson have the same amazing zest to
find pleasure in everything? Or make pleasure out of
nothing! Or did one have to be old before time became so precious, the need to make the most of it
inspired a creative talent for delight?

Her bedside telephone rang.

Maggie dropped the photograph back in the drawer
of her writing desk, shutting it away before answering
the call which would be from Sedgewick, telling her
the real live flesh-and-blood Beau Prescott was on the
last lap of his journey home. Her heart fluttered nervously as she picked up the receiver.

"He's earlier than we thought, Nanny Stowe."
Sedgewick's plummy tones rang in her ears. "Master
Beau does have a way of getting out of airports in
record time." A touch of pride there.

They all loved him; Sedgewick, Mrs. Featherfield,
Wallace, Mr. Polly. To them Beau Prescott was still
their wild child, grown to manhood admittedly, but in
no way changed from their long affectionate view of
him. They wanted her to love him, too, but that was
an entirely different ball game. To Maggie he was a
stranger, even though he was Vivian's grandson.

"Did Wallace say how far away they are?" she
asked.

"About twenty minutes." A lilt of excitement, anticipation. "I trust you are dressed and ready, Nanny
Stowe."

To knock Beau Prescott's eyes out. That was the

general advice. The plan. Consensus had been absolute—Mr. Vivian would have expected it of her.

"Yes, Sedgewick," she returned dryly. "But I think it best to give Master Beau time to greet you and Mrs. Featherfield before I intrude. After all…"

"Splendid idea! We'll hold him in the vestibule chatting. Then you make your entrance. I do hope you're wearing black, Nanny Stowe. It looks so well against the red carpet on the staircase."

Maggie rolled her eyes. "Yes, Sedgewick, I am wearing black," she assured him. "In mourning. Not for dramatic effect."

"Most appropriate," he warmly approved. "Though you must remember Mr. Vivian's principles, Nanny Stowe. You don't mourn a death. You celebrate a life. We cannot let sadness get in the way of…uh…propelling the future forward."

"Thank you, Sedgewick."

Maggie put the receiver down and heaved a long sigh, needing to relieve some of the tightness building up in her chest. She wandered around the room, trying to work off her inner agitation. Then on impulse, she opened the French doors that led onto the balcony and stepped outside.

The view drew her over to the balustrade. It was beautiful. Maggie doubted there was a more splendid position than here at Vaucluse, perched above Sydney Harbour, the magnificently kept grounds and gardens of Rosecliff spreading down to the water's edge in geometrically patterned tiers, each one featuring a fountain to delight the eye.

The mansion itself was a famous landmark for tourist cruises on the harbour. Built on a grand scale in the neoclassical style and set on five acres of prime real estate, its gleaming white-glazed terracotta exterior with its graceful Ionic columns and other lavishly decorated architectural features made it stand out, even amongst a whole shoreline of mansions. It seemed rather ironic that Vivian had made his fabulous fortune from parking lots. From the most practical of properties to the sublime, Maggie thought.

He'd taken enormous pride in what he'd privately called the Prescott Palace, using it as it should be used for splendid charity balls and fabulous fund-raising soirees. She mused over the marvellous memories Vivian had given her. He'd loved showing off his home, loved the pleasure it gave to others simply by coming here, enjoying the wonders of great wealth.

But nothing went on forever.

Nothing ever really stayed the same.

Maggie checked the time on her watch. The last bit of leeway for her was running out. She looked up at the cloudless blue sky, then down at the sparkles of sunshine on the water.

If you're out there somewhere, Vivian, and you really want this plan to work, you'd better start waving your magic wand right now, because fairytales just don't happen without it. Okay?

The only reply was the cry of gulls and the sounds of the city.

Maggie took a deep breath and turned to go.

The welcome mat was out for Beau Prescott.

CHAPTER THREE

THE huge black wrought-iron gates that guarded the entrance to Rosecliff were wide open. Wallace slowly turned the Rolls-Royce into the white-gravelled driveway, giving Beau plenty of time to get an eyeful of his home and its surrounds. As always, everything looked meticulously cared for; the lawns manicured, the rose gardens in healthy bloom, the two wings of the massive H-shaped mansion reaching out to welcome him.

It was nine o'clock and from the row of cars in the parking area for the daily staff, Beau realised nothing had been changed since his grandfather's death. The life here was flowing on as usual, waiting for him to come and make decisions. It made him doubly conscious of the responsibilities he had inherited.

Many people were employed on this estate, not only those who most concerned him. He suddenly saw the wisdom of the one-year clause in his grandfather's will. It would probably take that long to sort out what should be done with the place. Beau couldn't see himself adopting the lavish lifestyle enjoyed by his grandfather, yet it would be a shame to see Rosecliff become less than it was under some other ownership.

Wallace drove around to the east wing which housed the entrance vestibule. He stopped the car directly in front of the great double doors, distinguished from all the other doors by a frame of elaborate wrought-iron grillwork. They were being opened, with meticulous timing, by Sedgewick.

Sure the insidious Nanny Stowe would be standing right behind the butler, Beau didn't wait for Wallace to do his ceremonial chauffeur stuff. He let himself out of the Rolls and strode straight for the meeting which had become paramount in his mind.

To his somewhat bewildered frustration, it didn't happen.

She wasn't there.

Sedgewick, as imposing as ever, his big dark eyes somehow managing to look both doleful and delighted, took his hand in both of his in a fulsome greeting. "Welcome home, sir. Welcome home."

"Sorry not to have been here before, Sedgewick," Beau said with feeling, knowing how devastating it must have been for the old butler to lose the master he'd loved and been so proud of serving.

Then Mrs. Featherfield, dabbing the corners of her eyes with her trademark lace handkerchief, her well-cushioned bosom heaving in a rush of emotion. "Thank heaven you're here at last, Master Beau. It's a sad, sad time, but it lifts our hearts to see you home again."

"Dear Feathers..." His boyhood name for her slipped out as he gave her a comforting hug. "I truly believed my grandfather would live to a hundred. I wouldn't have been gone so long if..."

"I know, dear." She patted him on the back and eased out of his embrace to address him earnestly. "But you mustn't fret. As Mr. Vivian would say, yesterday's gone, and we have to make the most of today because tomorrow's just around the corner and time does slip by on us.''

He had to smile. ''I remember.''

''And I'm sure Nanny Stowe will fill you in on...''

''Ah, yes! Nanny Stowe.'' Beau pounced. ''Wallace has been telling me about our new addition to the household. Where is she?''

Sedgewick cleared his throat. ''A lady of deep sensitivity, Master Beau. Since Mrs. Featherfield and I have considerable longevity of service, Nanny Stowe wanted to give us a few minutes alone with you. However...'' He gestured towards the stairhall. ''...I expect she will be coming down any moment now.''

''Yes, indeed,'' Mrs. Featherfield got all fluttery, urging Beau forward, leading the way under the lofty Palladian arch to where the staircase rose in elegant curves to the second-floor hall. ''Nanny Stowe is so looking forward to meeting you.''

No more than he was, Beau thought darkly.

As he stepped into the majestic stairhall, his gaze automatically travelled up the flight of broad steps that gradually narrowed to the first landing. A woman stood poised there, framed by the tall, arched balcony window, the light beaming in behind her seeming to set her hair aflame; glorious red-gold hair that sprang alive from her face, fanning out like a fiery halo with long glittering streamers which rippled down past her shoulders.

Beau was so stunned by this vision, it took him several moments to recollect himself enough to register more than the fabulous hair. She had skin so white it looked translucent, like the most delicate porcelain. Her face was strikingly beautiful, every feature finely balanced to please. Her neck looked almost unnaturally long, yet it, too, seemed utterly right, purposefully proportioned to hold such a face, as well as being the perfect foil for the glorious wealth of her hair.

She moved, jolting his gaze down to her feet to check he wasn't imagining what he was seeing; feet encased in black shiny shoes with a gold chain across each instep; delicately shaped ankles leading to legs in sheer black stockings; legs that went on forever, mesmerising in their long, sleek femininity.

Beau knew there were sixteen stairs from the landing to the floor and she'd come down half of them before his eyes reached the short skirt of her black dress. A gold chain curved from hipbone to hipbone, dangling over her stomach, just above the apex of her thighs.

The air Beau was breathing started to fizz. Or maybe he wasn't breathing at all and suffering from lack of oxygen. His chest felt seized up and his heart was drumming like a bongo on carnival night.

He dragged his gaze up past an impossibly small waist. A wild phrase leapt into his dazed brain...breasts like pomegranites...lush and ripe and delectable. Then he knew he was getting light-headed because his blood was all rushing down to his groin and very shortly he was going to be in big trouble.

Get back to the pure loveliness of her face, some shred of sanity shrieked. As his thigh muscles tightened to contain the hot prickling of desire, he watched the fascinating rise of a flush creep up the pearly white skin of her throat and its subsequent spread to her exotically slanted cheekbones. Then he was looking into her eyes, eyes as blue as the waters of the Caribbean, dazzling in their blueness.

"Nanny Stowe, sir," Sedgewick announced, as though he were presenting the queen.

Not even the identification jolted Beau out of his enthralment. She was stepping towards him, no longer on the staircase, and he realised she was almost as tall as he was. If he reached out and pulled her against him their bodies would be right for each other, fitting together without any manoeuvring. The thought sent another shot of excitement down to the area Beau was struggling to control.

"Please accept my deepest sympathy, Mr. Prescott."

Her soft, sexy voice caressed his spine into a sensual shiver.

"Your grandfather's death was a grievous shock to all of us. I'm sure it was very much so to you."

He belatedly noticed her hand extended to him. He grasped it, seeing its slim whiteness disappear, enfolded by his own darkly tanned hand, her fingers fluttering slightly against the strength of his. He wrenched his gaze up to hers again, fighting the fascination of the seemingly fragile extension of her femininity within his grip.

He had to think, had to speak. This woman, unbelievably, was Nanny Stowe. Sedgewick had said so. Therefore she had to be, however incredible it was.

"Wallace told me how well you arranged the funeral," Beau heard himself say in a reasonably normal voice. "I could not have done better for my grandfather. Thank you."

She nodded towards Sedgewick and Mrs. Featherfield. "Everyone helped."

"Yes." Beau forced himself to acknowledge them. "It was a grand effort and I appreciate it. Very much."

They nodded, gratified.

Nanny Stowe spoke on, her sympathy subtly shifting to eloquent appeal. "I hope you don't think it...well, unseemly...but I felt you might like to share the paying of last respects to your grandfather, so I arranged for the funeral service to be videotaped. The cassette is in the library, should you want to play it through sometime."

"It was a kind thought. Thank you again."

Beau was happily drowning in the glorious blue of her eyes, sucked right in by their seductive softness and going down for the third time. He was barely conscious of the replies he made, words dribbling out of his mouth when called for. When she fell silent he didn't really notice. Her eyes were locked on to his and he could have stood there, getting in deeper and deeper but for Sedgewick interrupting.

"We have refreshments waiting for you in the informal dining room, sir."

Her hand twitched in his, making Beau realise he was still hanging on to it. Reluctantly he let it go. Her skin was like warm silk as it slid away from his. "Yes. I could do with some coffee, Sedgewick," he answered, obviously needing something to snap him out of this entrancement. Perhaps jet lag had caught up with him. Even moving from where he was didn't occur to him.

Sedgewick orchestrated action. "Nanny Stowe, if you'd like to lead the way…"

She took a deep breath as though she, too, was feeling a lack of oxygen. "Perhaps you'd like to freshen up first, Mr. Prescott."

Did he look as though he'd been run over by a truck? He smiled to dispel any questions about his mental and physical state, preferring to be the only one knowing how shaken he was. "No, I'm fine. Please lead on."

He was happy to stay behind her, watching her walk. Her fabulous hair reached almost to her waist, its gleaming ripples shifting with each step she took. It was so *alive,* Beau fancied there was an electric current running through it, throwing off showers of sparks that were infiltrating him. Something had to account for the weird pins and needles attacking every part of his body.

Though the jaunty roll of her very cute bottom below her impossibly tiny waist might be causing the itchy feeling in his hands. He kept them rigidly at his sides to stop them from reaching out. This woman would have to be the most stunningly gorgeous, sexiest creature he'd ever seen in his life.

And she was *Nanny Stowe?*

A sharply unsettling question darted through the fog in Beau's brain.

What had his grandfather been doing with her?

Two years she'd been under this roof and his grandfather, according to Wallace, had definitely not fallen into his second childhood. The more Beau thought about the situation, and all he'd heard and seen so far, it became disturbingly clear that Wallace, Sedgewick and Mrs. Featherfield viewed Nanny Stowe as mistress of the house.

And she was playing hostess to him right now!

The bottom suddenly fell out of the excitement she'd stirred in him. Beau went cold all over. It made horribly perfect sense. His grandfather had always enjoyed having a pretty woman on his arm. On both arms. But having found *this one,* why bother with any other? She had star quality on a megascale and his grandfather would have adored parading her everywhere. And probably adored her, as well! He'd loved owning beautiful things.

Beau's stomach started contracting, working up a nauseous feeling. Refreshments were certainly in order. He obviously needed food as well as coffee.

When they reached the informal dining room, his suspicion was further confirmed by the way she moved automatically to the foot of the table and Sedgewick held her chair for her. Clearly it was her place and taken for granted, even though his grandfather was no longer here.

Then Mr. Polly arrived on the scene, carrying a basket of freshly cut, dark red roses. His weather-beaten face was cracked into a benevolent smile. "I'm so sorry I missed you at the front doors, sir. Good to have you home."

Beau shook the offered hand. "Thank you, Mr. Polly. The gardens look as superb as ever."

"I keep at it, sir. I brought this basket up. Thought Nanny Stowe might like to put these roses in your room, sir." He turned to her. "They're the best of the Mr. Lincolns, Nanny Stowe. Lovely fragrance."

She blushed.

Beau was once again distracted by the fascinating flow of colour lighting up her pale skin.

Mrs. Featherfield swooped. "I'll take the basket, Mr. Polly. Let's go out to the kitchen and put the roses in water. Nanny Stowe will see to them later. She's having coffee with Master Beau right now."

Yes...they all considered Nanny Stowe a cut above themselves, Beau thought, watching Mr. Polly being swept away. Arranging roses in a vase for a guest's room was the kind of genteel occupation suited to the mistress of the house. Except he wasn't a guest. Which probably accounted for her embarrassment. She knew, even if the others didn't yet appreciate it, his arrival changed the status quo.

Sedgewick proceeded to serve them with coffee and a selection of freshly baked croissants. "If you'd like something more substantial, sir, Jeffrey, the cook, is standing by."

"No, I did have breakfast on the plane, Sedgewick. This is more than enough, thank you."

Sedgewick stationed himself by the sideboard, ready to be attentive to every need. Nanny Stowe composed herself again, adopting a waiting attitude. Beau ate a crisp croissant and drank some coffee to wash down the flaky crumbs. It didn't really help his churning stomach but it gave him time to think.

"Did my grandfather call you Nanny Stowe?" he asked.

A wry little smile played on eminently kissable red lips. "It amused Vivian to give me that title, Mr. Prescott."

The familiarity of *Vivian* hit him in the gut. "So it was a pet name," he suggested.

She frowned. "Not exactly. It did have a sort of purpose. My job was to be with him, accompanying him wherever he wanted to go and generally looking after him. But he didn't call me Nanny himself. I was always Maggie to Vivian."

"Maggie..." he repeated, knowing it plucked at a chord of memory.

"Yes. My Christian name is Margaret, you see."

Maggie, the cat. That was it! Maggie from one of his grandfather's favourite movies, *Cat On A Hot Tin Roof*. Elizabeth Taylor had played the role. She was married to a guy whose wealthy old father was dying and to clinch her husband's inheritance she had pretended to be pregnant.

Pregnant!

Beau's mind suddenly billowed in horror at the next thought that filled it. He'd more or less challenged his grandfather to beget his own heir for Rosecliff. While his grandfather hadn't actually married Maggie Stowe, she'd lived very cosily with him for two years and she'd been given a year's grace here after his death...which could mean his grandfather had still been hoping for a result.

"More coffee, Nanny Stowe?" Sedgewick asked, holding out the coffeepot.

She shook her head. Was she being careful of her caffeine intake?

"More coffee, sir?"

He waved it away. His heart was beating so fast he didn't need any artificial stimulant. And thinking of hearts reminded him his grandfather had died of a heart attack...*before anyone expected him to!*

Doing what?

Trying to father a child?

Beau looked down the table at the blue-eyed red-haired siren who had power enough to entrance a man into attempting any reckless stupidity.

He had to know.

He had to ask.

He tried to find a way of couching the question less shockingly. Somehow the sense of urgency mashed his brain. Nothing came but the bald need to get the issue resolved. Immediately! The words shot out of his mouth...

"Are you pregnant, Maggie?"

CHAPTER FOUR

SEDGEWICK dropped the coffeepot.

The shock of this extraordinary happening momentarily distracted Maggie from the deeper shock delivered by Beau Prescott. She stared down at the broken pot and the coffee spreading across the parquet floor with a sense of disbelief. She'd never known Sedgewick to drop anything. Every one of his movements was a study in grace and dignity. Had he been as stunned as she was by the outrageous question thrown at her?

"I do beg your pardon," he intoned, his face quite blank, as though he couldn't believe the mishap, either.

"I'll get one of the maids to clean it up," Maggie said, pushing her chair back for action.

"No, no…I see I have been splashed, as well." Distress showing now. For Sedgewick it was quite impossible to tolerate any imperfection in his dress. "I shall have this…this mess…seen to immediately. Please excuse me, sir, Nanny Stowe."

Maggie was left to face Beau Prescott alone. She stared at him down the length of the table, her mind skittering over the wild hopes she'd been nursing. If he imagined her pregnant, to some other man…he couldn't be feeling as overwhelmed by her as she was by him. Which put her hopelessly at odds with the feelings he'd stirred in her.

Never in her life had she been hit so forcefully by sheer male sex appeal. When he'd entered the stairhall and looked up at her on the landing, she'd been stunned into immobility by how little the photograph had represented the real man. His skin glowed with vitality. The streaks of sunshine in his hair had gleamed like gold. His face wasn't just strongly handsome. His eyes were so magnetic they made it instantly charismatic.

His physique was no less impressive. Casually dressed in khaki shirt and trousers, he seemed almost larger than life, like a throwback to when men were hunters and survival of the fittest meant something. If his grandfather had been the ultimate sophisticate, Beau Prescott was the prime male animal, throwing out a compelling challenge to his female counterpart on some instinctive level that had nothing to do with civilisation.

She had no idea how long she'd stood on the landing, enraptured by him, but when she had finally willed her legs to move, the nylon in her tights seemed to crackle with electricity, sending little quivers of sensation through her thighs. Even more shockingly, she'd felt the hot moistness of sexual excitement as he watched her descend the stairs, his gaze travelling slowly up the length of her body until even her breasts started tingling and tightening in rampant response to the primitive charge emanating from him.

Then the mad joy of finding he was taller than she was, tall enough to make her feel they were made for each other. And his hand taking hers, like a burning brand on her skin, a claim of possession, of mating. Utter madness in the light of the question that was still ringing in her ears and echoing around the emptiness it had opened up in her brain.

And he had seemed so nice, as well. Charming. She could have sworn the attraction was mutual...the way he'd absorbed every detail of her appearance, gazed into her eyes, held her hand. She'd been dizzy with exhilaration by the time she'd sat down at this table. Then with Mr. Polly's suggestion of putting roses in Beau Prescott's bedroom, she'd begun fantasising...

Maggie swallowed hard. She had probably needed a sobering slap in the face. The dynamic green eyes were still intensely focused on her but she found them uncomfortably piercing now. He was waiting for her reply. Not that he had any right to it—such a personal thing to ask!—but she felt pressed to clear the air between them.

Her tongue felt thick. She forced herself to produce a flat statement of fact. "The answer is no, Mr. Prescott. I'm not pregnant and not likely to be."

He looked relieved.

Maggie was goaded to ask, "Would you mind telling me what possessed you to make such an inquiry?" She couldn't help a somewhat terse note creeping into her voice. Disappointment, most probably. Or disillusionment. She must have been fooling herself over his reaction to her since he had jumped to the conclusion she was intimately involved with someone else.

He winced. "My grandfather wanted an heir."

Confusion whirled. "Aren't you his heir?"

"Yes." A heavy sigh ending in a rueful grimace. "But he was on at me to get married and have a child to safeguard the family line. The last time I was here with him, I suggested if he was so keen to pass on his gene pool he should have a child himself.''

Enlightenment dawned like a white frost, covering and killing what had seemed like warm fertile ground between them. ''You thought...that I...and Vivian...'' Maggie choked. It was too awful a lump to swallow.

He at least had the grace to look discomforted. ''It seemed...possible.''

''Vivian was in his eighties!'' There'd been almost sixty years between them!

''A man's libido doesn't necessarily wear out with age,'' came the dry observation. He offered a crooked smile. ''And you are very beautiful.''

Maggie was not mollified. She knew perfectly well that beauty was a learnt skill. Vivian had taught her that. He'd seen the raw potential in her and taken pride in developing it. However, beauty was not really the point at issue here. Beau Prescott was horribly mistaken in his judgment and he had to be corrected. She eyed him with searing determination as she spoke.

''Even if Vivian had felt...that way...about me, and he didn't...''

''Maggie, you exude sex. No man would be proof against it, not even an octogenarian.''

''Oh!'' Her face started heating up again. ''You're terribly wrong.'' It was Beau himself who exuded sex, not her. No other man had ever made her feel so sexually aware of herself. It wasn't fair of him to transfer what had happened between them to anyone else. She tried to explain. ''Vivian liked me. He was proud of me...''

"I have no doubt he adored you. From your feet up."

"He didn't want me like that!" she cried in exasperation, barely holding back the burning fact that Vivian had wanted her to want *him!* And the terrible truth was she did. Except he wasn't turning out as nice as she'd first thought him.

Blatant scepticism looked back at her.

"Your grandfather was a gentleman," she declared emphatically. Which was more than she could say for him, the way he was going.

"My grandfather enjoyed flirting with young women," he countered. "He insisted they kept him young. He boasted he'd live to a hundred. He brings you into his home and he dies at eighty-six. From a heart attack. Having met you, what am I supposed to think, Maggie?"

Her stomach revolted at the image he conjured up. Her eyes flashed fierce resentment at his offensive line of logic. "A man of any sense might have made some discreet inquiries before leaping to unwarranted conclusions," she threw at him.

"Hardly unwarranted. It wouldn't be the first time a beautiful young woman connected with an elderly millionaire. Power and wealth are well-known aphrodisiacs."

"Right!" Maggie snapped, furious with his cynical view of a relationship which had been precious to her. "I suppose you envisage me just lying back, closing my eyes and thinking of Rosecliff!"

"And all that goes with it."

Her heart lurched. Hearing Vivian's own words, though they had applied to a possible marriage to his grandson, touched a very raw place. The whole idea of *giving it a chance* with Beau Prescott suddenly became intensely repugnant to her. Mutual attraction did not suffice. He would see her as a gold-digger even if he was panting after her.

The cleaning brigade came in, two of the daily maids whose job it was to keep every room in a pristine state. Maggie greeted them and introduced them to their new employer. Apart from those few words she waited in seething silence while the mess was attended to. Beau Prescott also held his tongue, which was just as well, because she felt like biting it off.

Of course, Vivian's wealth had made life easy for her, and Rosecliff was the most beautiful place in the world to live in, but she wouldn't have come here if she hadn't liked Vivian Prescott, genuinely liked him, and she certainly wouldn't have stayed if he'd tried to come on to her. No way! She would have been out of here like greased lightning!

The maids left, their efficiency truly admirable. Probably the thick atmosphere in the room had hastened their work. Maggie braced herself for the task of setting Beau Prescott straight. In no uncertain terms!

He spoke first. "I like to know what I'm dealing with, Maggie."

"My title is *Nanny* Stowe." And she hadn't given *him* permission to call her Maggie.

"Nannies do tuck their charges into bed," he dryly pointed out.

"Not...this one," she retorted in high indignation.

He shrugged. "It seemed best to be direct. Your relationship with my grandfather..."

He stopped as Sedgewick stepped into the room, bearing another coffeepot.

Maggie was so incensed with Beau Prescott's *directness* she swung around in her chair and impulsively appealed for backup. "Sedgewick, Mr. Prescott wants to know if I was sleeping with his grandfather. Would you be so kind as to…"

The butler halted in horror. The hand holding the coffeepot shook alarmingly. Maggie held her breath, silently cursing herself for shocking the poor man again.

"Steady, Sedgewick," Beau Prescott gently advised.

The elderly butler stared at the treacherous hand until it performed as it was supposed to, holding firmly. Then he raised his eyes to the ceiling, as though appealing to the heavens beyond it. The expression on his face was easily read. What was the world coming to?

"I'm sorry for upsetting you, Sedgewick," Maggie said remorsefully.

"Not at all," he said with lofty dignity. He carried the pot to the sideboard, set it on the hotplate with due ceremony, then swung around to face *the wild child* with a look of pained reproof. "Sir, Mr. Vivian did not have an illicit liaison with Nanny Stowe," he stated unequivocally.

"Thank you, Sedgewick," Maggie leapt in before Beau Prescott could open his big mouth. "Did you ever see him kiss me other than on the cheek or on the forehead, or, in a moment of pure old-world gallantry, on the hand?"

"Never!" came the emphatic reply.

"Did you ever observe him fondle me in what could be called an intimate manner?"

"Certainly not!"

"Did he ever display any sign of being a randy old man around me?"

Sedgewick looked affronted, as well he might. "Mr. Vivian was a gentleman." Which, to Sedgewick, was the definitive reply, delivered in ringing tones.

However, since a similar declaration by her had not cleared Beau Prescott's prejudice, Maggie continued to have the situation spelled out, her eyes glittering a proud challenge at her accuser at the other end of the table.

"In your own words, Sedgewick, what was Mr. Vivian's manner towards me?"

"I believe he thought of you as his adopted daughter whose company was always a delight to him."

"And my manner towards Mr. Vivian?"

"You wish me to be frank, Nanny Stowe?"

"Ruthlessly frank, Sedgewick."

"I believe you thought of Mr. Vivian as a benevolent godfather who made beautiful things happen. You saw it as your job to make them even more beautiful for him."

The truth. The simple truth. And it had been beautiful. It was wicked and destructive of Beau Prescott to soil it with his revolting and insulting interpretations. A rush of tears blurred her eyes and clogged her throat. "Thank you, Sedgewick," she managed huskily.

He bowed to her in a show of respect. "At your

service, Nanny Stowe. Would you like your coffee cup refilled?''

''Please.''

He handled the pot perfectly. Not a drop wavered or spilled. The masterly performance provided a sense of calm. ''A refill for you also, sir?' he inquired.

''No. I've been refreshed enough for now, thank you. Refreshed and reassured that my house is in very clean order. For which I thank both of you.''

His dry tone spurred Maggie to look at him again. He gave her a mocking glance as he rose from his chair and she knew instantly he still held suspicions about the innocence of her relationship with his grandfather, despite Sedgewick's prime witness statements. However, he wasn't about to comment any further on it at this point. He addressed himself to Sedgewick, his manner briskly purposeful.

''I trust my luggage has been taken up to my room?''

''Of course, sir.''

''Good. I'll be off for the day as soon as I've showered and changed clothes. Please warn Wallace to have the car standing by.''

Maggie felt impelled to say, ''If I can be of any assistance...''

His eyes glittered at her. ''You are not *my* nanny, Maggie.''

Which swept the mat out from under her feet and left her feeling miserably hollow.

''I daresay I'll see you at dinner tonight, taking your usual place,'' he went on.

''If you'd prefer I didn't...''

"On the contrary, I'll look forward to the pleasure of your company."

He was plotting something. She could feel it. With malice aforethought. Every nerve in her body was twanging a warning.

He started to leave, then paused, looking back at her, a sizzling challenge in his eyes. "Oh, and don't put roses in my room, Maggie. I am not my grandfather."

CHAPTER FIVE

BEAU stood under the shower, willing the hard spray of water to beat out the sexual edginess Maggie Stowe had implanted. The woman was a witch. His grandfather had obviously been enchanted by her and she had Sedgewick curled around her little finger, too. Not to mention the rest of the household staff; Wallace singing her praises, Mr. Polly bringing her roses, Mrs. Featherfield star-struck by her stunning beauty.

No doubt about it, she cast a powerful spell.

Beau savagely promised himself he would not fall victim to it.

She'd had him captivated at the start but he wouldn't go under like that again. He was wise to her now. Maggie Stowe was out for all she could get. If she thought she could turn him into another godfather, making beautiful things happen for her, she'd find herself frustrated at every turn.

It was bad enough that his grandfather had blindly doted on her. Beau was glad there'd been no physical intimacy between them. Not that he would have begrudged his grandfather the right to have his sexual needs satisfied. A man was a man, regardless of age. But taking a woman as *young* as Maggie Stowe was a bit much for Beau's stomach. She could only be in her twenties.

Though she certainly knew how to use her assets! No grass growing under *those* expensively shod feet.

The question was…how much hay had she made during the two sunshine years of prettily playing pet daughter to a besotted old man who had the means to indulge her every whim?

Making things more beautiful for him…huh! Making herself more beautiful with nice little items of jewellery would be her line. He'd bet his boots on it. Lucky his grandfather hadn't adopted her legally. A fine old mess that would have made of the will. As it was, she didn't have a leg to stand on in claiming anything apart from a year's free housing and wages.

Though God knew what she'd picked up in gifts while his grandfather was alive. Well, he was about to look into that. She'd invited him to make discreet inquiries before leaping to unwarranted conclusions. Little mistake there. Beau was going to make exhaustive inquiries and he didn't care whose feet he trod on in getting to the truth. If she expected him to be *a gentleman* of the old ilk, overlooking unpleasant little realities, she was in for a few nasty shocks!

He stepped out of the shower with all mental motors running. While he dressed he telephoned the family solicitor and the firm of accountants who handled his grandfather's finances, giving fair warning of an imminent visit from him. He didn't want condolences. He didn't want any pussyfooting around the situation. He wanted answers, and woe betide anyone who didn't have them ready for him.

The ride into the city from Vaucluse was accomplished in brooding silence. Wallace, possibly advised by Sedgewick to keep his mouth shut unless called upon to answer questions, offered no comment about anything, and Beau didn't care to have any interruption to the plan of action fermenting in his brain.

The solicitor's offices were in Philip Street. Once there, he told Wallace not to wait around. He'd catch taxis wherever else he wanted to go. Privately, he didn't want Wallace reporting his every move to *Nanny* Stowe.

Beau was ushered straight into Lionel Armstrong's executive suite, greeted warmly by the man himself, and offered refreshments which he declined. They sat in leather chairs across a magnificent mahogany desk and Beau tried to repress the feeling he was dealing with a self-satisfied man who needed stirring.

Lionel Armstrong was just a bit too sleekly well-fed for his liking. The man was in his fifties, handsome in a heavy-set way, vainly proud of his thick white hair which was carefully styled and groomed, and he made almost a fetish of the trappings of success.

"Well, Beau, I'm happy to say there are no tricky problems with your grandfather's estate. Vivian made a straightforward will and the process towards probate is in hand."

"I'm glad you consider it straightforward, Lionel. I consider it somewhat surprising. Firstly, I thought he would have made more provision for those who had been with him longest."

"Ah, you mean the faithful four. No need for concern on their behalf. Sedgewick, Mrs. Featherfield, Wallace and Mr. Polly have been well taken care of. Your grandfather set up superannuation funds for them. John Neville, the head accountant can fill you in on those. I believe the settlement for each one after the stipulated year is up will be well into six figures.''

''And Margaret Stowe?''

''The nanny?'' Lionel looked amused.

Beau was not amused. ''Yes. The nanny who has a year's grace along with the others.''

''Oh, that was one of Vivian's little quirks. Wouldn't be talked out of it. Said the others depended on her to do the right thing. And I must say she did a splendid job of organising the funeral. Splendid!''

''The cost of which was claimed against the estate?''

''Of course. Everything in order. All accounts checked. If you're going to see John Neville, he'll show you.''

''Fine. Does Nanny Stowe have a superannuation fund, too?''

''Every permanent employee on the estate has. It's the law. However, since she'll only be in service for three years altogether, it will not amount to much. Nothing there for you to worry about.''

''I'd like to see her file.''

Lionel frowned. ''What file?''

''You know and I know my grandfather kept a file on all his employees. References, résumés, and any other information that seemed pertinent. It was your responsibility to run a check on them. For live-in staff taking up positions of trust, it was a mandatory precaution.''

''True.'' His mouth twisted over the word. He leaned back in his chair, linked his hands across his stomach, and viewed Beau with a wry expression. ''I have no answer to the mystery of Margaret Stowe.''

Beau's sense of anticipation turned into unpleasant tension. "What the hell is that supposed to mean?"

"Ask me for a file on anyone else and I can supply it. All I can give you on Margaret Stowe is a copy of her birth certificate. It states she was a foundling. The informant is a doctor and apparently he gave an estimated date of birth. No parents. No witnesses."

"Where did her name come from then?"

"Perhaps a note was pinned to the baby. Perhaps the doctor or a nurse gave it to her. Nobody knows. The doctor died eight years ago. He operated from a home surgery. The house burnt down and all his medical records were destroyed. That line of investigation came to a dead end. As did every other line." He unlinked his hands to gesture helplessly. "It was as though Margaret Stowe lived in a vacuum until her meeting with your grandfather."

"Oh, come on. You expect me to believe that?" It was looking like a straight case of dereliction of duty to Beau.

"It's the truth," came the hasty assurance.

"You must have put a private investigator onto her," Beau pressed, not prepared to accept a white-wash.

"With zero results. Apart from her birth certificate, she had no official existence. She had never filed a tax return, never owned a credit card. No record of education or employment..."

"What about social security? She could have been raking in unemployment benefits."

"She was not listed on any register. No passport. No driver's licence. I assure you, every avenue of information was thoroughly checked. More than once.

When the first investigator failed to uncover anything, I hired another. With no better outcome.''

Someone has always kept her, Beau thought. She's probably had a string of godfathers since her teens.

Lionel Armstrong shrugged off the failure. ''Her known life began the night Vivian met her and offered her the job as his nanny.''

''Well, she very conveniently sprang alive then,'' Beau commented acidly. ''How did he meet her?''

''He said she was selling roses.''

Beau barely refrained from rolling his eyes. Maggie Stowe had done her homework on Vivian Prescott. He'd been her mark and he'd fallen for her; hook, line, and sinker.

''What did my grandfather say when you put it to him that you could collect no background on her?''

''He laughed and dismissed it as of no importance.''

Lionel Armstrong's *laissez-faire* attitude niggled Beau. ''Didn't you argue with him? Point out the dangers?'' he accused more than asked.

''Naturally. But to no effect. Your grandfather did have a mind of his own, Beau, and there was no changing it on Margaret Stowe.''

Bewitched, Beau thought broodingly.

''In fact, he said something I've never forgotten,'' the solicitor went on musingly. ''And I must say, he did seem to have taken on a new lease of life.''

''What were the unforgettable words?' Beau demanded tersely, unable to suppress his frustration over getting nothing tangible to hang on Maggie Stowe.

''I think Vivian revelled in her nonentity status. He said, '''She's going to be my creation, Lionel. And very possibly my salvation.'" And his eyes were twinkling in that impish way he had."

"Salvation?"

The solicitor shrugged. "Your guess is as good as mine. Maybe he thought he'd found an angel."

"If she sprouts wings, I'll start believing it," Beau said caustically. He'd had enough talk of angels.

"Disturbs you, does she?" The solicitor eyed him with speculative interest.

"I don't like mysteries," Beau growled.

"Well, perhaps being such an experienced explorer, you'll dig it out."

Beau intended to, one way or another.

After he left the solicitor's office, he stopped at a street café to grab some lunch and chew over what he'd learnt so far. Which wasn't much. Maggie Stowe was twenty-eight years old and she was the only one who could tell him about herself. It would probably be a stack of lies he'd get from her but at least he could have the lies checked.

He'd blundered in being too direct this morning, putting her offside. He would have to smooth that over this evening, lull her into feeling he accepted her at face value. It would be stupid to give offence again. Better to charm the information out of her. Let her think she was winning.

He thought briefly of dropping in at the head office of the travel agency he'd established in Australia. It was hardly urgent. Helen Carter had been running the business efficiently for the past three years. It was a courtesy to tell her he was back home again, but it could wait another day. He was too obsessed with

Maggie Stowe to give Helen or anything else his undivided attention.

The firm of accountants was housed in the MLC building, right in the city centre. With clients as wealthy as Vivian Prescott, they could well afford such premises. Beau thought of all the parking stations and lots his grandfather owned—*he* now owned—around Sydney. With traffic the way it was, and ownership of cars always on the up and up, the business of providing parking was probably the most solid investment of all in a fast-moving world.

Beau had no intention of interfering with it. John Neville and his associates had been handling the family finances for many years and were very proficient at it. They earned their fees. Beau had no doubt everything would be in order on the business side. It was his grandfather's personal expenses over the past two years that interested him, particularly in regard to their connection with Maggie Stowe.

John Neville was happy to oblige him with this information. He was a small, neat, precise man, proud of his meticulous bookkeeping. For some reason, Beau found Neville's bald head reassuring. His gold-rimmed spectacles also seemed to add an air of no-nonsense professionalism.

"Miss Stowe's salary was generous." He pointed out the figure from the wages book. "But, as you can see, not outrageously so, considering she was always on call. Never had days off."

"Never?"

"Not even a vacation. Vivian took her everywhere with him and he paid for what he called her appearance clothes out of his own pocket. Naturally, he used credit cards. Everything he bought for Miss Stowe to wear has been itemised.''

He passed over a detailed printout for Beau to peruse. Dresses, suits, hats, shoes, handbags...practically all designer wear if the steep cost was anything to go by.

''As you know, your grandfather enjoyed a very full social calendar with his many charities and he liked Miss Stowe to shine at his side.''

''From the look of this, she certainly shone. What about jewellery?''

''Rented for any big occasion. Miss Stowe would not accept jewellery from your grandfather. In fact, she sold some of the evening gowns Vivian didn't want her to wear again and returned the price she got to us. All properly docketed. The accounts for the funeral were scrupulously kept, as well.''

''No discrepancies?'' Beau queried. His ''feathering her nest'' theory was being shot down and that didn't make sense to him.

''None,'' came the firm reply.

''Nothing missing?'' Beau pressed.

John Neville looked uncomfortable. ''There is and there isn't. I find it very vexing. Nothing I could do about it but I strongly dislike not having everything accounted for.''

''Please explain,'' Beau encouraged, his interest sparked again.

''Oh, it has nothing to do with Miss Stowe.'' He beetled a frown over his glasses. ''Vivian could be a very wilful man. When he didn't want to take advice, he wouldn't.''

Beau had more or less heard the same from Lionel

Armstrong and the matter was very definitely connected to Maggie Stowe. He waited for John Neville to enlighten him further.

"He came in one day, about two months before his death, and asked me to get him a million dollars in cash."

Two months before his grandfather's death rang a bell in Beau's brain. That was when his last will and testament had been made...including Margaret Stowe.

John Neville pursed his lips in disapproval. "Now that amount of money one simply does not carry around in cash. Legitimate transactions are all paperwork. Naturally I inquired the reason for such a request."

"And the answer?" Beau prompted.

"He said it was his money and he could do what he liked with it and it was none of my business." The affront of that statement coloured John Neville's voice. "I could not shake him into telling me what he wanted it for. He stubbornly insisted I get the cash for him. I had no other choice. It was his money."

"Did you find out where it went?"

He dolefully shook his head. "I expected it to turn up. A purchase. A land deal. Something. I looked for it. I even asked around in certain circles. Very discreetly, of course. Not a trace, not a hint. I can show you the paperwork attached to the handing over of the million dollars to your grandfather. He took it. I have witnesses to his taking it. But what he did with it was, and still is, a complete mystery."

Beau now had two mysteries.

The case of the woman from nowhere.

The case of the missing million.

He also had a very strong conviction…find out the background of Maggie Stowe and he'd find the missing million.

CHAPTER SIX

MAGGIE stared gloomily at the vast array of very expensive clothes in her wardrobe. Vivian had made dressing up fun. She'd seen no harm in giving him the pleasure of it and there was no denying she had enjoyed feeling wonderfully glamorous, swishing around in gorgeous outfits.

She didn't think Beau Prescott was going to view any of this as fun, though. The money Vivian had spent on making her look splendid was sure to bring his grandson's censure down upon her head. He'd more or less accused her of being a whore this morning. Milking an old man's indulgence was bound to come next. She wished she could shrug it off, not care, but it hurt having Vivian's grandson think badly of her. It hurt all the more because she'd felt so instantly, so strongly attracted to him.

A knock on her bedroom door broke into her misery-laden thoughts. "Yes?" she called despondently.

Mrs. Featherfield came bustling in, brimming with excited anticipation. "He's home, dear. Sedgewick suggested predinner drinks in the salon at six-thirty. That gives you half an hour to get ready." She eyed the opened wardrobe with avid interest. "He's still in his suit so you could wear something really pretty."

Maggie grimaced. "It's no use, Mrs. Featherfield. He doesn't like me."

"Nonsense! Master Beau was well and truly bowled over this morning. Saw it with my own eyes."

"Well, he very quickly recovered and bowled me out of any getting together with him," Maggie said dryly.

"Now that's not it at all. Sedgewick and I agree that Master Beau liked you so much he got jealous at the thought of you and Mr. Vivian...being close. He wanted you for himself."

Maggie found herself at a loss as to how to argue with such triumphant satisfaction.

"So don't you worry, dear," Mrs. Featherfield rushed on. "Wallace said Master Beau was very quiet on the way into town. Sedgewick feels that setting the record straight about you and Mr. Vivian gave him food for thought and reconsideration."

All of it bad, Maggie figured, remembering the spark of malice in his eyes as he'd left her.

"Shock can do funny things to people," Mrs. Featherfield remarked with a wise look. "We all need a period of adjustment. Master Beau will have settled himself down by now and I'm sure he'll be charming to you this evening. You must give him another chance, dear."

He was going to make mincemeat of her. Still, if she didn't put on a show, Mrs. Featherfield, Sedgewick and the others would feel she was letting down the side. Maggie forced a smile. "I'll do my best."

The housekeeper beamed happily at this reassurance. As she hurried out of the bedroom she warned, "Six-thirty, mind. Jeffrey's cooking Beef Wellington for dinner and he's very particular about the timing."

No doubt there'd be romantic candles on the table, too, Maggie thought, her heart sinking at the prospect of bearing the cynicism in Beau Prescott's eyes. She hoped Sedgewick wouldn't suggest champagne. The foreboding words, *I am not my grandfather,* were still ringing in her ears.

In a spurt of defiance, Maggie pulled out her red poppy dress. Since Beau Prescott viewed her as a scarlet woman, she would throw it right in his face. She had nothing to be ashamed of in her relationship with Vivian and she'd be damned if she would let his grandson turn it into something it wasn't. Vivian had adored the boldness of her wearing red with her red hair, declaring it both daring and dazzling. Certainly the poppy dress would do away with any accusation she was not trying hard enough.

Maggie had always thought of it as a flirty little dress. It wasn't exactly figure-hugging. The silk chiffon with its vibrant pattern of scarlet blooms splashed over a white background, more or less slid and shifted over her curves, falling to a cute short skirt with an underfrill rippling softly around her thighs. At the back, the skirt was looped up at the centre to showcase rows of flouncy underfrills that took on a life of their own when she moved.

Definitely a flirty dress. One could even say it flaunted her femininity. With malice aforethought, Maggie proceeded to complement the dress with appropriate accoutrements; sheer, pale flesh-coloured tights, high-heeled red sandals that strapped up to above her ankles, and long, dangly crystal earrings to reflect colour as they sparkled against her hair.

She sprayed her neck and wrists with Christian

Dior's "Poison" for good measure, then pranced downstairs, all flags flying for the cause, although to her mind, the cause was already dead and beyond revival. Nevertheless, Sedgewick could not fail to be pleased with her appearance and any further debacle between her and Beau Prescott would not be laid at her door.

She swept into the salon, walking to the strong beat of rebellion. Sedgewick was serving her antagonist with a freshly made martini. Beau Prescott, standing in a commanding position in front of the French marble mantelpiece, above which hung a romantic painting of Cupid at play——definitely a perverse comment on what was going on here——took the martini from the silver tray, looked at Maggie who had paused to take in the scene, and gave her the full force of a brilliant smile.

Her heart tripped.

"Good evening, Maggie," he said pleasantly, lifting his glass a little as though toasting her appearance. "You make me see you would brighten any man's world, regardless of age or circumstance."

Unsure whether or not she had just received a compliment, Maggie seized on another implication in his greeting. "Did you have a difficult day?" she asked.

"Mmmh…" His eyebrows slanted musingly, attractively. "…I'd call it a three martini day. Will you join me in one? It may help smooth over my *faux pas* of this morning."

An apology? Maggie was dumbfounded. She'd come to do battle and here he was in retreat. A very graceful retreat, too. And he looked so heart-meltingly handsome, a twinkling appeal in his eyes, a smile still playing on his lips, the compelling power of his masculinity given a tantalisingly civilised veneer by a perfectly tailored three-piece suit.

Her mind belatedly dictated a "Yes, I will, thank you," reply, and a smile to match his. With Sedgewick looking on benevolently, she could hardly do anything else. Besides, she really did want to give Beau Prescott another chance, so long as he was being nice to her.

Maggie was instantly outmanoeuvred from adopting her usual hostess role. Beau Prescott took charge, very much the master of the house as he gave orders to Sedgewick, directed Maggie to sit on the sofa of his choosing and invited her to sample Jeffrey's hors d'oeuvres—his best creations—artistically arranged on an exquisite platter.

The little puff balls filled with creamed egg and topped with sour cream and caviar were irresistible. Besides, Maggie needed something to settle the sudden attack of flutters in her stomach. She was very, very conscious of Beau Prescott as he took the armchair closest to her, facing her across the oval end of the gilt-legged marble table which served both pieces of furniture.

He chose one of the fine pastry boats containing Jeffrey's special crab mixture. Undoubtedly, Sedgewick had instructed the cook to pull out all stops tonight. After all, it was Master Beau's homecoming. Maggie hoped it would be interpreted that way by the man who was now viewing her with speculative interest.

"I imagined you very differently, you know," he confessed with an appealing twist of irony. "I guess, because you were linked in the will with Sedgewick and the others, I automatically put you in the same age bracket. Or thereabouts.''

It was an understandable assumption. ''Then I must have come as a shock,'' Maggie offered, remembering Mrs. Featherstone had excused his behaviour on that basis. She was prepared to be as generous.

He nodded. ''To put it mildly. I'd be grateful if you'd fill me in on a few things that have been teasing me all day.''

''What do you want to know?'' Maggie asked warily, willing to meet him halfway if this was a genuine offering of goodwill.

''Well...'' He gestured helplessness. ''How did you come here? Did my grandfather advertise for a nanny?''

The questions sounded like pure curiosity, nothing judgmental about them. Maggie's nervous tension eased a little. Such curiosity was fair enough in the circumstances.

''I don't think the idea had even occurred to him until after he'd met me,'' she answered, shaking her head as she remembered back. ''I'm sure it was just one of those things that grew on him and he kept adding to it as he went along.'' Wanting Beau Prescott to understand she looked at him appealingly. ''It was like a game to Vivian.''

''To you, too?''

Maggie felt she was on trickier ground here. She answered cautiously. ''He made it fun. But he taught me a lot, too.'' The sense of loss welled up in her again. ''Your grandfather was a wonderful person and he gave me the best years of my life," she said in a burst of fierce feeling.

The intent green eyes seemed to probe her emotion, measuring it. Maggie's nerves tensed up so much she was almost driven to challenge any disbelief he had, but she held her tongue. She couldn't make him believe her. He either did or he didn't.

Luckily Sedgewick picked that touchy moment to serve her the martini she'd agreed to have and Maggie gratefully grabbed the glass, hating the searching silence. She gulped some of the strong liquor, barely stopped herself from choking on it, then sought further distraction in selecting one of Jeffrey's dainty pizza circles with cheese, tomato and olives baked into it.

"I know what you mean," Beau Prescott said quietly, startling her into looking at him again. His expression was soft, fondly reminiscent. "He had such a zest for life it was infectious. He opened windows to the world for me."

"Yes. Oh, yes! That was just how it was." The words tripped out, surprised delight lifting her heart.

His head tilted inquiringly. "How did the two of you meet?"

She relaxed into a smile. "It was the most amazing encounter. I was out of work at the time and just scraping a living by peddling single roses. I bought them at the markets, and prettied them up with foil paper and ribbons. I did the rounds of fancy restaurants in the evening and a lot of guys would buy one for the woman they were dining with. A romantic gesture, you know?"

He grinned. "How much did you charge?"

She grinned back, pleased he didn't disapprove of her enterprise. "Five dollars. I figured for an elevation of mood, it was worth at least as much as a glass of wine."

"Perfectly reasonable," he agreed encouragingly. "I guess my grandfather couldn't resist buying one from you."

"Well, not exactly. He was with a large party of people at one of the restaurants I visited. Parties like that didn't usually buy so I was concentrating on the smaller tables. Twosomes were always more promising. Your grandfather must have been watching me because he caught my eye and beckoned me to his table. To my astonishment he insisted on buying the lot, every rose in my basket. He said a pretty girl should be partying on a Saturday night and I should sit down and join *his* party if I had nowhere better to go."

Beau Prescott laughed, his good humour wafting over Maggie like a seductive caress. "That sounds so typical," he said, his green eyes dancing at her, enticing her into telling him anything he wanted to know. "Whom did he have with him?"

"It was a group of artists who'd won awards."

"Anyone well-known?"

"I don't really know. I never met them again."

A slight frown.

"You could ask Sir Roland," Maggie suggested helpfully. "He was there. I guess it was an Arts Council thing."

"Ah!" The frown smoothed away. He smiled. "How many roses did you have left?"

"Twenty. For me it was a great sale. And then

being offered free food, too...I was only too happy to sit down and join them. I ended up having a marvellous time."

"My grandfather had a great talent for parties," he said fondly.

"He certainly loved being the ringmaster and he did it superbly," she warmly agreed.

They both sipped their martinis as memories lingered, their mutual affection for a grand old man subtly linking them and pushing their differences away. The silent hum of harmony filled Maggie's heart with pleasure. This is how it should be, she thought, and imagined Vivian smiling down at them.

Beau leaned over and helped himself to an egg and caviar puff. The movement instantly restirred her awareness of the man; the fabric of his trousers tightening across a width of thigh that looked so hard and strong, Maggie's breath caught in her throat as her mind flashed to how he might look naked, might feel against her own nakedness. She quickly shifted her gaze to his hand before a betraying blush erupted. It was just as fascinating in its maleness. A sure hand, she thought, capable of anything, and a little quiver of possibilities raced through her, further undermining her composure.

"So how did the nanny idea come up?"

The light, quizzical words shot through her ears and forced her to refocus. Maggie took a quick breath and almost gabbled in her haste to resume a natural flow of conversation.

"Oh, Vivian asked me about my life and I gave him a potted history, making it more colourful than it really was." She shrugged. "You know how you do with strangers whom you never expect to meet again. It's easier, more entertaining than laying out the less pleasant bits.''

''You mean you made up stuff?''

''No. What I said was true,'' Maggie rushed to assure him. ''I did travel with a circus…' The moment the word was out, Maggie caught her breath, looking to see if there was an adverse reaction. Some people considered a circus unsavoury.

No frown. If anything, an increase in interest. Maggie braved going on.

''I worked as a nanny for the family who owned it. I also worked as a nanny on an outback station. I've done lots of other jobs, as well, but those were the two that evoked the most interest the night I met Vivian.''

He looked bemused. ''What was the name of the circus?''

''Zabini's. It was a relatively small outfit, family owned and run. It toured country towns.''

''I would have thought that kind of thing was out of date now,'' he remarked.

She nodded in quick agreement. ''It was having trouble pulling in crowds when I was with it and that was over ten years ago. The problem was, the family didn't know any other way of life. I was only with them for one tour. They didn't need me after they went into recess so I don't know what happened to them.''

''And that's when you headed into the outback?''

''Yes.'' She smiled ruefully. ''It seemed like another adventure. I had experience as a nanny and there was plenty of employment available in that area.''

"Where did you end up?"

His obvious desire to know and the lack of any critical air released Maggie from caution. She happily painted the picture for him.

"On a big cattle station in the Northern Territory. A place called Wilgilag. Which means 'red' in the Aboriginal language. And it sure was. Red earth as far as the eye could see. Endless red. The cattle roamed over hundreds of square kilometres in search of feed. It was like another world. A different life."

She caught herself back from rattling on too much and waved a dismissive hand, consigning Wilgilag to the past. "It was all a long time ago. Lots of water under the bridge since then, but that was the background of the nanny business."

He smiled, obviously content with her explanation and amused by the situation. "I see how you could make it sound very colourful and my grandfather would have enjoyed it immensely. Did he latch on to you straight away for the nanny job?"

"No. I was really surprised when the party broke up and he gave me his card, saying if I wanted a steady job, to come and see him the next day."

"He didn't specify the job?"

She shook her head. "It made me wonder. But he'd been so charming. I'd liked him. And curiosity got the better of me. I couldn't see any harm in finding out what kind of job. I mean, I wasn't exactly doing anything wonderful, just making do until something interesting turned up."

"Then Rosecliff must have come as another surprise to you."

His eyes were twinkling, teasing, and his ready acceptance of everything she said was so exhilarating, Maggie didn't feel she had to watch her tongue or manner with him anymore. Her natural exuberance came bursting forth, eyes sparkling, hands flying, words bubbling.

"Was it ever! I couldn't believe anyone actually lived here at first. I thought I must have somehow got it wrong. Even after Sedgewick admitted me to the house—a real live butler, for heaven's sake!—and ushered me into Vivian's presence, it felt as though I'd stepped through the looking glass like Alice, and sooner or later something would snap me back to reality."

He smiled.

Maggie happily beamed a smile right back at him, not noticing anything amiss in his. The circus hadn't owned a tiger. She had never seen a live one. She had no point of comparison.

"What did you think of the nanny proposition?" he prompted, still smiling.

She rolled her eyes. "Wild! But just the thought of living here was wild. It was all so impossibly wild I couldn't resist giving it a try. After all, I could always walk away if I didn't like it. But it just escalated into something more and more wonderful."

He looked quizzically at her. "You didn't ever feel the lack of...well...younger company?"

She might have, if Beau Prescott had come home before this. He was very acutely reminding her she was a young woman with a whole stack of unfulfilled needs, clamouring to be met. There seemed to be a simmering invitation in his eyes. It kicked her pulse into such rapid action it was difficult to concentrate on giving him an answer to his question. She blurted out the truth.

"I was too busy to think of it."

"For two years?" he queried, his gaze wandering over her with a sizzling male appreciation that said more clearly than words she had been wasted in a limbo of nonsexuality.

Maggie's skin started prickling. She gulped some more of her martini and shoved a crab boat into her mouth, desperate to stop the rise of heat. She crossed her legs, inadvertently drawing Beau Prescott's attention to them, and wished she could uncross them again as she inwardly squirmed under his gaze. Afraid more leg action could only be seen as provocative, Maggie plunged into speech.

"I'd been in the company of heaps of young men before I came here. None of them were capable of giving me what Vivian did."

His gaze flicked up and there wasn't the slightest haze of warmth in his eyes. Two green shards of ice sliced into her, cold and deadly. "I don't suppose any of them were millionaires."

The comfort zone created by his earlier geniality was comprehensively shattered. Maggie felt a chill deep in her bones. He'd been putting on an act, drawing her out to get something bad on her.

"Apart from my salary, I never took any money from Vivian, Mr. Prescott," she stated, a bitter defiance edging her voice.

He let her denial hang for several moments before drawling, "I wasn't suggesting you did. But a lot of money was spent on you, Maggie. Your clothes..."

Her chin went up. "Yes and tickets to the opera,

the theatre, concerts, balls…you name it, Mr. Prescott, and I certainly was given a free ride to all of them. No question. I'm guilty of going along with everything Vivian wanted. And I'm guilty of loving it, too. I'm sorry it sticks in your craw so much. Maybe you'd like to ask Sedgewick for another martini. Make it four for the day.''

She set her own glass on the table and stood up, bristling with angry disillusionment. ''Shall I ring for him to come?''

He waved a dismissive hand and tried an appeasing smile. ''I was merely remarking on the obvious. Why take offence?''

''You could have tried looking beyond the obvious, Mr. Prescott.''

The pretence of a smile twisted into a grimace. ''You call my grandfather by his first name. Why not use mine?''

''Because I don't assume familiarities. I never have. In my experience it's asking to be slapped down if you do,'' she answered tersely.

''Oh, come on! Not in Australia,'' he protested. ''It's the most egalitarian society in the world.''

''That depends on where you're coming from,'' she mocked. ''You've never lived an underprivileged life, have you? Never had to learn to be subservient. You have no idea what it's like to live that kind of life.''

He frowned, unable to deny the charge.

Sick at heart, Maggie turned away from him and walked around the table, moving to stand where he had stood earlier, in front of the fireplace. She felt too agitated to sit down again. She glanced up at the painting of Cupid frolicking in a garden and a rueful smile curled her lips. The arrows being shot here to-night weren't dipped in a love potion. More like poison.

When she swung around, Beau Prescott was keenly observing her, a perplexed V drawing his eyebrows together.

"I'll tell you what Vivian gave me," she shot at him. "Acceptance, approval, liking, respect. He took me in and made me one of his family. He transformed me into something more than I was and showed me what was possible. He educated me in so many ways—books, music, art—opening my mind to things I'd never known and would never have learnt without his guidance and tuition."

She paused, showing her contempt for his shallow judgment of the situation. "I don't know why your grandfather did it. Perhaps he was lonely. Perhaps he enjoyed playing Henry Higgins, turning me into 'His Fair Lady.' Perhaps he liked having an eager pupil. And I was certainly that. I was hungry for all he gave me and I did my best to live up to all he wanted for me."

Her sense of rightness urged her to add, "I'm not ashamed of that, Mr. Prescott. I'm proud of it because I did Vivian proud. I loved your grandfather. I really did. And whether you like it or not, that's the truth."

He said nothing, retaining an intense air of listening as though waiting to hear more. She held his gaze in fierce challenge. The silence lengthened. The tension between them thickened.

Sedgewick stepped into the room and cleared his throat. "Dinner is ready, sir."

It was so pedantic, such a ridiculous anticlimax,

Maggie broke into a peal of laughter. "I do assure you, Mr. Prescott, our cook's Beef Wellington will be much tastier than sinking your teeth into me. Best that we answer his call immediately."

She set off for the dining room, not waiting for any response, savagely berating herself for being a gullible fool. Never again, she vowed. Beau Prescott might be capable of charming birds off trees, but this bird was going to keep her wings tightly folded against him.

CHAPTER SEVEN

BEAU forced his jaw to keep working, doggedly chewing up each mouthful of the Beef Wellington to the point where he could swallow it. At the other end of the table, Maggie Stowe was carving through her dinner with military precision, and he'd be damned if he was going to let her see she'd robbed him of his appetite. The woman had too much power as it was.

She tapped straight into every male hormone he had, setting them more abuzz than they'd ever been, regardless of the dictates of his brain. She messed with his mind, too, blurring what should be completely clear, straight-line logic. He couldn't decide whether she was a superb actress or completely for real. If it wasn't for the missing million, he'd be tempted—strongly tempted—to accept her story at face value.

At least he now had some facts to check. Sir Roland would be a reliable eyewitness to the first meeting in the restaurant and he wouldn't mind Beau questioning him about it. Zabini's Circus and the cattle station, Wilgilag, were items he could pass on to Lionel Armstrong. Any competent private investigator should be able to get some character references out of them. *If* she'd told the truth about her *nanny* background.

He glanced down the table. Her face was in shadow, frustrating his need to see past her polished facade. "Sedgewick, would you please switch on the overhead light and remove the candelabra? I can hardly see what I'm eating."

"As you wish, sir."

Beau could feel his irritation growing as Sedgewick complied with ponderous dignity. The disapproval emanating from the old butler was so thick it could be cut with a knife. Maggie Stowe was clearly upset. With all the subtle skill at Sedgewick's command, he kept letting Beau know who was at fault and it wasn't the nanny.

The brighter illumination of the room didn't really help. Maggie's face was like a white mask, completely expressionless. Beau watched her pick up her glass of claret and take a swig. Not champagne tonight, he thought with acid satisfaction. He'd told Sedgewick to serve a good red. The champagne days were over for Nanny Stowe at Rosecliff. No doubt she could buy it for herself soon enough with the missing million.

She had to have that million squirrelled away somewhere.

It was the obvious answer.

Yet she had flatly denied taking any money from his grandfather apart from her wage. And she had scorned him for not looking beyond the obvious.

The woman was a wretched torment. He glared at her as he picked up his glass of wine, needing a good dose of full-bodied claret to ease the angst she'd given him. She didn't look up from her dinner. Since she'd sat down to it, she hadn't met his gaze once. Beau was left with the strong impression she had wrapped a shield around herself and comprehensively shut him out. Her stony silence reinforced it.

The urge to smash it down spurred him into speech. "What did you do after you left Wilgilag?"

Very slowly, reluctantly, she lifted her head. Her eyes glittered like sapphires. "If you want ammunition against me, find it yourself, Mr. Prescott," she said flatly.

Her reply gave him no joy nor satisfaction. Having made him feel like a slime, she returned her attention to her meal and continued eating. Beau couldn't stomach any more food. She had his gut twisted into knots.

"I simply want to know more about you, Maggie," he defended, trying to beat off the sense of being in the wrong. Very badly in the wrong.

She shook her head, not bothering to even glance up at him.

Beau seethed with frustration. He couldn't make her talk. He recalled the artless, open way she had bubbled on before he'd put in the jab about millionaires and savagely wished he'd held his tongue on that point.

Yet had it been artless or artful? Truth or lies? Impossible to know until he'd checked out what she'd told him. One thing was certain. Because of his stupid gaffe in revealing his own train of thought, she was not about to hand him any more information about herself.

He emptied his glass and signalled to Sedgewick to refill it. The action was performed without comment, without eye contact. Beau felt himself being cold-shouldered on more than one front.

Was he wrong about Maggie Stowe? Was he hope-

lessly, foolishly, hurtfully wrong? He couldn't deny
that her passionate defence of her relationship with
his grandfather had struck chords of truth. And guilt.

Perhaps he'd been lonely.

Those words hit hard. Beau doubted this situation
would ever have arisen if he hadn't stayed away so
long. Or if he'd found the time and the woman to
marry and have children—which was what his grandfather had most wanted, an extension of the family
line. Having plenty of friends did not provide the
same sense of closeness and caring as having someone
who belonged to you, who was there all the time.

Beau could even see now why his grandfather had
chosen to take Maggie Stowe in and make her one of
his family...a flower-seller with the potential to be
much more, given the means and the guidance.
"She's going to be my creation," he'd boasted to
Lionel Armstrong, and he would have revelled in the
role of Henry Higgins; the achievement of it, the sheer
theatre of making someone over and producing a star,
the heady reward of her appreciative response to his
teaching.

If Maggie Stowe had really had an underprivileged
life, why wouldn't she be eager to try everything on
offer, hungry for it, loving it? It made sense. The only
fly in that ointment was the missing million, which
suggested she could be a very clever con woman.

Beau just couldn't let that go. Not without knowing
more. A lot more. He cursed himself again for letting
his advantage slip. She was on guard against him now.
He'd have to work other angles and hope something
pertinent would turn up.

It startled him out of his dark reverie when she rose

abruptly from her chair. She laid her refolded napkin on the table and looked directly at him, making his heart kick at the renewed link between them.

"I beg to be excused, Mr. Prescott," she said with quiet dignity. "I am not feeling well."

Which left him no loophole for insisting she stay. Beau set his glass down and rose to his feet, courtesy demanding he let her go gracefully. "I'm sorry. If there's anything you require…"

"No. Thank you." She turned to the butler. "Sedgewick, please apologise to Jeffrey for me. I know he will have prepared a special sweets course. Perhaps Mr. Prescott will have two helpings to make up for my leaving it."

"I'll ensure Jeffrey understands, Nanny Stowe," Sedgewick returned kindly, drawing her chair back for easier movement.

"Thank you."

She walked the length of the table with the carriage of a queen, yet when she paused by Beau, he saw she was trembling, and her face was so bloodless he wondered if she were really ill. Her eyes were no longer glittering. They reflected a sickness of soul that screwed Beau up even further.

"I've been presuming too much. I won't sit at table with you again, Mr. Prescott. As you said this morning, you are not your grandfather."

Beau opened his mouth to argue, everything within him rebelling against the evasion she intended. The mystery of her was not resolved. He wanted the challenge of her presence. He wanted more of her than he could admit to. But before he could voice the words

of protest tumbling through his mind, her eyes misted
with tears, making him recoil from saying anything.

"Goodnight," she whispered huskily and moved
on, walking briskly from the dining room, leaving him
feeling like a monster for making her cry.

He watched her go, the flouncy little frills of the
sexy red dress taunting him with what she might have
given him if he'd acted differently. His loins ached
with thwarted desire. His mind raged against the circumstances that trapped him into keeping his distance.
The angry frustration welling up in him could barely
be contained.

Sedgewick proceeded to clear her end of the table,
apparently unconcerned by the incident, carrying on
with his job, transferring her plates and glass to the
traymobile. Beau, still on his feet, his napkin crum-
pled in his hand, glared at the old butler for being so
deliberately officious about his duties.

"If you've got something to say, Sedgewick, spit
it out!"

A dignified pause. A slight raising of eyebrows. A
look down his noble nose at Beau. "I was thinking,
sir, I have served many people in my years at
Rosecliff. Amongst them, the high and mighty of this
country, one might say. People who thought their
wealth or power put them above others. Nanny Stowe
may have come here without much to recommend her,
sir, but she is a genuine lady. Mr. Vivian certainly
thought so, too."

"You don't know what I know, Sedgewick," Beau
retorted in dark fury.

His lofty mien became ever loftier as he answered,

"Possibly not, sir. I have only had two years' close acquaintance with Nanny Stowe."

Which neatly sliced Beau's feet out from under him. He threw the napkin on the table, picked up his glass and strode to the sideboard to collect the decanter of claret. "Please inform Jeffrey I won't be wanting sweets, either. Nor anything else tonight, thank you, Sedgewick," he said in savage dismissal.

"Very well, sir."

Armed with what was left of the good red he'd insisted upon, Beau headed for the library, haunted by a glorious mane of red hair, a red dress that was too damned bold to be worn by a woman with that shade of hair, and the authoritative words of a man who should know what he was talking about.

He found the videotape of his grandfather's funeral and slotted it into the machine ready to play. Left to himself, he automatically shed the constraints of formality, taking off his coat, vest and tie, then rolling up his shirt sleeves and undoing the collar button. Getting rid of his excess clothes, however, did not ease his pent-up tension.

He poured himself a glass of wine, picked up the remote control panel, and tried to find some comfort in one of the leather armchairs. His thumb was hovering over the play button when he realised his anger was inappropriate for watching the funeral of a man who'd raised him from boyhood, a man he'd revered and loved.

He waited a while, occasionally sipping the claret, clearing his head of Maggie Stowe and filling it with memories of happy times with his grandfather; the adventures they'd had together—cruising The Great

Barrier Reef, seeing the wildlife of Kakadu National Park, exploring the underground world of Coober Pedy—then in his teens, the trip to Europe where his grandfather had made history come alive for him.

It had been Vivian Prescott's gift, to make the world a marvellous place. And he'd chosen to bestow this gift on a woman he'd picked up one night. Right or wrong, it had been *his* choice. *His* choice, too, to take a million dollars and do whatever he'd done with it.

Beau wanted to respect those choices. He really did.

A genuine lady...

God! He even wanted to believe Sedgewick was right!

He just couldn't bear the thought his grandfather had been fooled.

With a heavy sigh, Beau pressed the play button and set the footage of the funeral rolling.

He found the service intensely moving...the songs, the words spoken, the roses, the cathedral packed to overflowing by those whose lives had been touched by Vivian Prescott. Then, at the cemetery, it was indeed a fine, fine touch, having a piper in full Scottish dress, lead the carrying of the coffin to the graveside, the age-old wail of pipes ringing down the last curtain.

The final ceremonial words floated past Beau unheard, his attention fastened on the little group of people standing a few metres behind the bishop, his grandfather's family, for lack of anyone closer.

He was inexorably drawn into studying the woman who had most recently come amongst them, the woman at the centre of his grandfather's last years.

He focused his entire mind on setting aside his prejudices and seeing her as objectively as he could.

She looked magnificent in a tailored black suit and a broad-brimmed black hat that managed to be both sober and stylish. *Doing Vivian proud,* Beau thought, finding himself admiring her stance, despite his suspicions about her character. Not once did she look down at the grave. She held her single rose clutched to her chest, and her face was lifted to the sky.

She didn't appear to be aware of the tears trickling down her cheeks from the corners of her eyes. Or she determinedly ignored them. She kept her gaze fixed upwards, as though she wouldn't let herself believe Vivian Prescott was in that coffin. His spirit was out there somewhere, soaring free, not tied to the earth in any shape or form. The Angel of Death had come kindly...

Beau winced at the thought, yet ironically found himself in sympathy with it. He switched off the video, having seen enough. His glass was empty but he didn't feel like drinking more anyway. The sense of having done Maggie Stowe an injustice was strong. Even if she'd had her eye on the main chance, capitalising on all she could, she certainly hadn't failed her benefactor at the end.

I loved your grandfather. I really did. And whether you like it or not, that's the truth.

He might not like it, but Beau was beginning to believe it. The whole funeral was an act of love, getting it right, doing his grandfather proud. He could no longer see it as putting on a show. There was too much care, too much feeling behind it for him to dismiss as an exercise in showmanship.

So where did that leave him? An unappreciative, ungrateful, blundering clod? Driving a woman to tears instead of giving her her just due?

Wretchedly at odds with himself, Beau pushed out of his armchair and paced restlessly around the library. He'd set about this nanny business all wrong, shooting off with bees in his bonnet, right from the start, making assumptions without the evidence to back them up.

What if Maggie Stowe was *a genuine lady,* as Sedgewick claimed?

He'd virtually accused her of being a whore and a gold-digger. There could be no doubt he was wrong on the first count. As to the second...God only knew!

She'd gone off to her room in obvious distress because of him. His grandfather had installed her in a position of respect here and he'd cast her as unworthy of it, cross-examining her like a criminal in the hot seat and judging before she'd had a proper hearing. Was that fair? Would his grandfather be proud of him?

Shame wormed through Beau. His grandfather had trusted him to let everything at Rosecliff carry on as dictated in the will and he hadn't even let one day pass without blowing it apart. Not one day. What he personally thought was irrelevant. This was a matter of trust to be kept, and keeping it was the least he could do since he hadn't been here to do more when it would have truly counted.

He checked his watch. It wasn't too late to straighten things out with Maggie Stowe. Best to do it right now. That way they could start afresh tomorrow. And he'd get to go to bed with a clear conscience.

Fired with resolute purpose, Beau left the library, only realising when he was halfway up the stairs, he didn't know where Maggie Stowe was. A moment's thought gave him the answer. His grandfather would have given her the Rose Suite. Their relationship had begun and ended with roses. It fitted. And whatever his grandfather had ordained for her, had to be carried on for a year, come what may.

CHAPTER EIGHT

MAGGIE didn't want to answer the knock on her door. It was bound to be Mrs Featherfield, anxious to smooth things over again, offering excuses and pleading for more time and tolerance, probably bringing a soothing cup of hot chocolate to settle her down. Impossible mission, Maggie thought, inwardly recoiling from having to cope with it. Better to ignore the knock. She'd done enough answering.

She stayed out on the balcony, ending more than the long day of emotional battering. Her life with Vivian...Rosecliff...this view over the harbour...she had to say goodbye to all of it. There was not going to be any flow-on with Beau Prescott.

Another knock, louder, more insistent than before.

Maggie frowned. Was her silence giving Mrs Featherfield concern? She didn't want to worry the housekeeper. Sedgewick would have reported the scene in the dining room to her and she might start thinking of real illness if she wasn't answered. Better to let her check and have done with it.

Reluctantly but resignedly Maggie moved back to the French doors and called, "Come in," hoping a minute or two would see the end of any fussing.

Beau Prescott stepped into her bedroom.

Disbelief dizzied her. Shock hit in waves. He'd actually come after her, right into her room, invading her privacy, making nowhere at Rosecliff safe from him. The civilised veneer had been cast off; his suit-coat, vest and tie gone. She was swamped by his sheer maleness, the physical dominance of the man, the aggressive masculinity that seemed to swirl from him and draw on her like a powerful magnet.

She stared at his muscular forearms, bared to the elbow as though ready for action. Her heart skittered. She wrenched her gaze up but it moved erratically over his chest, finding the arrow of flesh where his shirt was opened and fastening on the base of his throat where the throb of his pulse was clearly visible. Another shock. Tension tearing at her, forcing her to lift her eyes to his, to see what was driving his heart faster.

A blast of raw desire plastered her with a hot awareness of what she was wearing. She hadn't thought of it, her mind scrambled by the impact he was having on her. The slinky nightgown had been a personal purchase, its sensual appeal irresistible, a clinging creation of navy silk and lace that slid over her skin and snugly moulded her breasts.

It wasn't transparent and Mrs Featherfield had seen and admired it, but the lace-trimmed V neckline revealed more cleavage than she would normally put on public view, especially to Beau Prescott who already saw her as having no morals at all. It didn't stop him looking at her with lust, though, and Maggie felt a quite vixenish satisfaction in stirring him on a primitive level when he couldn't possibly approve of himself being attracted to her.

Rebellion simmered through the heat he aroused. She'd be damned if she'd make any move to cover up. She was in her own bedroom. She enjoyed wearing this nightgown. It was one little pleasure he couldn't take away from her. Besides, a belated attempt at modesty wouldn't impress him. He thought badly of her anyway. So let him stare. Let him burn as much as she was burning.

Her breathing quickened with the reckless, dangerous excitement of challenging him on the most basic level of all. She felt her breasts rising, falling, straining against the flimsy silk, her nipples hardening, flaunting themselves through the provocative arrangement of lace. And she didn't care. She revelled in the feverish glitter in his green eyes, exulted when splashes of red speared across his cheekbones betraying *his* rush of blood, *his* discomfiture with what was happening to him, *his* response to the stimulus of her femininity.

Her mind boiled over the memory of her first sight of him this morning, the sizzle of sexual awareness, the pleasure, the tingling anticipation of thinking they were made for each other, the sense of at last having found a man she wanted, with whom it would be right to mate. Frustration seethed through her as her eyes raked down his body. This man should have been hers. Her bones ached with the sense of loss.

"Maggie…"

The low, gutteral uttering of her name snapped her gaze up to his again, violent emotion coursing through her at the violation of possibilities he'd ripped away before they could grow. Damn him! she thought in bitter fury. Damn him for not recognising what should have been!

It was true…*Hell hath no fury like a woman scorned.* But he wasn't scorning her now. Not now.

Whatever barriers he'd imposed between them were gone and *the wild child* had been let loose. Except there was no child in those blazing eyes. It was rampant manhood on the move and he was coming at her, tearing off his shirt, blinding her with a broad expanse of bronzed masculinity.

His clothes were dragged off and hurled away with lightning speed. No hesitation. No inhibitions. Maggie did nothing, said nothing to stop him. She was totally mesmerised by the splendour of the nakedness emerging. He was stunningly beautiful and compellingly, enthrallingly, majestically *male*. Her whole body was seized by an intense lust for the touch of him, the taste of him, the complete and utter experience of him.

She'd barely had time to want when the want was answered, a strong, binding arm scooping her against him, the thin film of silk between them heightening the physical sensations of their bodies meeting, impressing, exulting in the intimate contact, his hand burrowing under her hair to curl around the nape of her neck, and his mouth crashing onto hers, hot and hungry, intent on plunder.

He kissed her deeply, a strong, sweeping possession determined on tasting all of her. Electric tingles shot straight through the roof of her mouth and exploded any inhibitions she might have had. A fever of passionate need took hold, inciting a wild response to his aggression. They ravished each other in a tumult of kisses, laying an erotic siege that pushed for more to give under the urgent escalation of the desire to take everything—everything they could—here and now.

His fingers hooked into her hair, tilting her head back to expose her long throat to a burning trail of kisses, and she arched into him, loving the sensation of hard unyielding thighs against hers, the thick roll of his manhood pressing into her stomach, the heave of his chest compressing her breasts.

He dragged the shoulder straps of her nightgown down with his teeth, then lifted her off her feet, one arm under her thighs, the other under her back, lifting her high, shoulder high, draping her over his arms like a taut bow, her naked breasts pointing up for his mouth to take, the swell of her flesh taut and tingling, drowning in fierce waves of pleasure from the hot suction of his kisses as he carried her across the room.

Then the bed was beneath her and the silk was stripped from her body, leaving her open and utterly vulnerable to the eyes glittering down in rapturous thrall. "The same colour...the same colour..." he murmured, his voice furred with sensual satisfaction, and he thrust his fingers through the red-gold silkiness at the apex of her thighs, parting it, sliding down to caress the soft, intimate folds it hid...hidden no more as he buried his face there, tasting her sex, driving fierce spasms of sensation through her, making her jerk and twist and tremble with the intensity of his pleasuring.

She felt herself poised on a perilous edge, her muscles melting, contracting in need for him to be inside her, filling the aching emptiness, easing the screaming desire for full possession. She was dying for him...dying for the proving of the promise, the final plunge that would make order of chaos. She clawed at his head, silently begging, urging him to come to her.

He lifted himself over her, kissed her, his mouth

invading hers with fast, darting thrusts that drove her wild, taunting her with what he withheld. She bucked in fierce incitement and he rolled, carrying her, lifting her to straddle him, challenging her to take what she wanted, how she wanted. He was there for her, primed and positioned, and his hands slid to her buttocks, squeezing them, urging her into aggressive action.

She took him, lowering herself slowly, feeling herself stretching to encompass him, feeling her muscles convulse around him in response to the exquisite sensation of him moving into her, deeper and deeper, like a delicious fullness pushing through a long swelling stem to a place that seemed to blossom with soft inner petals opening to ecstasy.

She closed her eyes, focusing on that fantastic inner world, and she lifted herself, revelling in the reverse slide, wanting to feel it all over again, exulting in the control he'd given her. His hands stroked up her back and lifted her hair forward, over her shoulders. As she undulated over him, he curtained her breasts with the long silky tresses, caressing them through the soft, tantalising texture in the same rhythmic movement she used on him, evoking a wild eroticism that drove her into pumping faster, until suddenly she was shaking, unable to direct anything.

He whirled her onto her back and took command, poised over her with all his dominant power and the stroking inside her was different now, like a steam train charging towards some zenith she couldn't even imagine, the rails sparking with showers of electricity—speed, power, action—and a scream of achievement building, building, rushing through her, pushing her to an incredible peak and bursting into an explo-

sion of intense melting sweetness that fused their
bodies together and left them collapsed on each other,
saturated in heat, all energy pooled and drained.

Maggie had no idea how long they stayed like that,
limp and damp and dazed in the aftermath of passion.
Eventually Beau dragged himself aside and lay on his
back, apart from her. She didn't mind the separation.
Her brain was in some strange limbo where thoughts
could not be defined, let alone caught and held. Somehow what had happened was too much to grasp, too
difficult to sort out. It hadn't really been she who had
shared in all those wild actions. Some kind of madness had possessed her.

As though this recognition and acknowledgment
cleared the haze a little, various ideas darted through.
The madness was his fault. He had incited it. After
all, she had never done anything like this before.
Though it shook her that she'd let it happen, in a way,
she had actually wanted it to happen. However, wanting him was no excuse when she knew perfectly well
his wanting would stop right here in this bedroom.

He didn't like her.

And she didn't like him, either.

So what on earth were they going to do now?

The silence and stillness stretched on, humming
with an awareness which was no longer sexual but
gathering just as much electric tension. However ex-
hausted they were, sleep was definitely not in the air.
Maggie suspected Beau Prescott was nursing the very
same thoughts that were plaguing her.

"It's been a long time since I've been with a
woman," he said at last, making it a quiet statement
of fact, all emotional judgment strained out of it.

He hadn't turned to her, hadn't moved at all. He spoke to the ceiling. Maggie understood this. It was easier to converse without looking at each other. The excuse he offered sounded reasonable enough for her to use, as well.

"Same here," she answered, speaking just as carefully. "With a man, I mean," she added for clarity.

"I didn't come in here to do that." A trace of shock in his voice.

"I didn't expect you at all." Maggie was pleased to make that point. "I thought it was Mrs Featherfield knocking."

Another silence, not quite so tense, carrying more a stunned quality which they both accepted now they had spoken. Maggie thought how strange it was... both of them sprawled stark naked on the bed, yet wrapped in separate worlds, despite the incredible intimacies there'd been between them. Clothes didn't seem to matter. Nothing could cover up what they'd done together. It felt ridiculous to even try.

"I watched the funeral," he said.

"Oh!" Maggie puzzled over why that was relevant in the current circumstances. "I hope it was all you would have wanted for your grandfather," she said gently, wondering if grief had knocked him sideways.

"Yes."

At least she had done something right in his eyes. Though it was a bit late to change anything between them.

"I wanted to tell you...wanted to apologise for my attitude today," he said in a rush. "I should have respected the position my grandfather gave you. And I will," he added determinedly.

Maggie gave it some thought but couldn't see how it would work, given his predilection to always thinking the worst of her. "I was planning to leave tomorrow," she stated bluntly.

She could feel him frowning. It took him a while to reply. "I don't want to drive you out." It was said stiffly.

He didn't really want her here, either. He'd made it perfectly clear their connection tonight was a total aberration. As it was for her. She found it difficult to even look at facing him tomorrow.

"It's best I leave. You needn't worry I'll take much with me. I tend to travel lightly and most of the clothes Vivian bought me won't fit into my usual life. You can sell them. The accountant, John Neville, will tell you where."

"But it's right for you to stay," he argued, uncomfortable with the outcome of his gold-digging accusations. It stirred him to move. He propped himself up on his elbow and frowned down at her. "It's in the will. My grandfather wanted it."

Even with a beetling frown on his face, he was an incredibly handsome man. But looks weren't everything. Sex wasn't, either. With a heavy sigh, filled with disappointment and resignation, she stated the reality she had faced earlier.

"Vivian is gone. You made me realise that today."

He expelled a deeper sigh. "I'm sorry. I don't know what else to say. Except I do want you to stay."

She searched the shadowed green eyes, trying to see what was driving him now. Was it only the will? Was tonight's cataclysmic folly influencing him? Was he thinking he might want more of her? Horror suddenly billowed through her mind. She jackknifed up, sitting with her hands clapped to her face before jerking around to face him with the dreadful truth.

"You didn't use protection!"

He shot up from an elbow to a hand prop. Her shock was echoed in his fast retort. "You're not on the pill?"

"No. I had no reason to be."

"Hell!" He thumped his forehead with the heel of his palm.

Maggie was struck by visions of him having explosive one-night stands all over South America. "Are you safe? I mean...medically clear of..."

"Damned right I am!" He whipped away the hand that had slid from his forehead to pinch his eyes. "Are you?"

"Yes. I haven't had sex for years!" she defended hotly.

The green laser beams retracted into dark turbulence. "Is there a chance of...of your falling pregnant?"

Maggie took a deep breath and calculated. It was the worst possible time. Which had probably contributed to the mad wanting to mate with him. Didn't they always say that was the danger period for women to fall to temptation?

"Yes. I'm afraid there is," she said flatly, scarcely able to believe she had been so stupid, so wilfully, wantonly stupid.

"Bloody hell!" he said, not liking it any more than she did. He swung his legs off the bed and sat hunched away from her, his head in his hands.

Maggie drew up her knees, hugging them, feeling more alone than ever.

The silence was filled with pregnant things.

"Well, you can't leave now," Beau said tersely, twisting around to direct his decision at her. "Not with this hanging over our heads."

Like the sword of doom, she thought, her heart sinking on the horns of their dilemma. She met his eyes, schooling herself to expect nothing. "Would you want the baby if I had one?" she asked, hating the idea of forced acceptance.

"Of course, I would!" He stood up, stiff with indignation. "Do you think I'm the kind of man who'd abandon his own child?"

People did.

Who knew that better than she?

Maggie never would. She couldn't. Impossible for her to trust anyone but herself to do right by her child. If she had one.

"I don't know you," she said. "I only met you today and you certainly haven't struck me as someone I could trust and depend upon. I think you'd do what suits you."

"Well, you're wrong," he declared, affronted by her opinion of his character. "And there's plenty of people who'd back me up on that."

She shrugged noncommittally. "I guess time will tell."

"Yes, it will."

He left her with that dark comment as he walked around the room collecting his scattered clothes.

Maggie sagged into dismal despondency. Maybe God would be merciful and let her get away with this one night of madness. When she did have a child she wanted to be in a true love relationship where abandonment would never be a possibility. She had no idea what kind of father Beau Prescott would make. Probably a resentful one and what good was that?

She didn't look at him. Didn't want to. In her mind he'd moved from being a possible mate to one who'd hate a lasting connection with her. Yet if he had fathered a child on her she couldn't shut him out of their lives. Not if he wanted in. She couldn't deprive her child of its natural father, couldn't let it feel abandoned by him.

"It's settled then," he said decisively, having gathered up his clothes and hung them over his arm, still careless of his nakedness. The green eyes held steely resolution. "You stay, Maggie. At least until we find out if you're pregnant."

"Yes," she agreed. It was the only sensible course to take.

Trapped, she thought.

Satisfied the matter *was* settled, he left, shutting her door on the most regrettable episode of her life.

CHAPTER NINE

BEAU leaned back against the door to the Rose Suite and shut his eyes in sheer anguish at having committed the worst folly of his life.

Trapped!

Trapped by the oldest method in the world.

Impossible for him to shun a woman he might have made pregnant. What's more, if she had his child he was tied to her for life!

And he'd walked right into it like one of those suicidal animals—lemmings—that threw themselves off cliffs. No rationality to what he'd done. No stopping for wiser consideration. His brain had fused and animal instinct had taken over the driving seat. He should have shot himself in the foot before going into Maggie Stowe's bedroom. It might have kept him sane.

Summoning up the last shreds of his utterly depleted energy, he pushed away from the door and plodded down the corridor to his own suite. One hell of a day, he thought, and hell's fires were still burning. He'd be damned lucky if he wasn't scorched forever from this night's work. Never in his life had he lost his head so completely. Never! He had no answer to it.

Sweet relief to reach his own bedroom and crawl between the sheets. He was wrecked. In every sense. Maggie, the cat, had clawed him inside out and finished up with a dish of cream that would never run dry...if she was pregnant and carried it through. Which she would. Beau had no doubt about it. The way she'd checked his attitude about fatherhood made that course a certainty.

Not that he'd want her to sneak off and have an abortion. His child was his child. Getting rid of it was not an option in his book. All the same, he desperately hoped there would be no consequences from tonight's madness.

In all fairness to Maggie Stowe, he couldn't say she'd planned it. There was no way she could have anticipated his visit to her suite. He had to believe her claim that she hadn't expected to see him, so she hadn't set out to seduce him by wearing the sinfully provocative slip of silk and lace.

No, she definitely hadn't planned it, but she was a dead-set opportunist. Why else would she have flaunted herself in a sizzling challenge to him? It was a carnal come-on if ever he saw one. No protest from her when he'd responded to it. No attempt to stop him. She'd been right with him from the start, revelling in the whole mad ride.

For a moment, his body gripped with the memory of how fantastic it had been, the incredibly intense excitement of... But it still shouldn't have happened. Giving great sex was fine but it wasn't all he wanted in a woman. For the mother of his child he'd want a few other attributes, especially someone he could *trust!*

And what did he have in Maggie Stowe?

A woman from nowhere!

Still, worrying about what couldn't be changed

wasn't going to get him anywhere, either. Sleep was what he needed. He'd face whatever he had to face tomorrow. Besides, there'd be time before the pregnancy deadline for him to get a handle on Maggie Stowe. She couldn't stay a mystery forever. The more he knew, the better equipped he'd be to make the right choices.

Beau blanked his mind and slipped into sweet oblivion.

The first day after *the night of the disastrous mistake* did not start well for Beau. Maggie failed to appear for breakfast. It was an ominous sign. They might have come to an understanding about her staying on at Rosecliff but goodwill had not been established. Sedgewick subtly let him know this was not a situation he favoured. The cold shoulder continued.

After breakfast, Beau took refuge in the library, a private domain where he could get on with his agenda for the day. He settled himself behind his grandfather's splendid mahogany desk—used more for the business of keeping his social diary and planning charity functions than anything else. The computer, fax machine and photocopier in the far corner of the room had also been used for these purposes but they were handy for Beau, as well.

Top priority was to telephone Lionel Armstrong and get another investigation started. Happily the solicitor was in his office and took the call immediately. Beau related the facts he now knew about Margaret Stowe and demanded immediate action. Urgent action. And reports coming in as fast as possible.

''I want those employers milked of everything they

know about her. Character references, background, even impressions if they don't have facts. Photographs, records…whatever can be dug up.''

"Beau…" A hesitation. ''…Is all this necessary? I mean…why go to town on her at this point? Is there good reason for it?''

Beau gritted his teeth. Good reasons abounded! Maggie Stowe might be the mother of his child. And there was still the missing million.

"Just do it, Lionel," he bit out.

A resigned sigh. "Vivian wouldn't listen to my advice, either. Makes me wonder what it is about this woman."

"The point, Lionel, is I want to *stop* wondering."

Beau had no idea when or how a pregnancy test could be taken but he had the strong feeling he shouldn't let the grass grow under his feet while he was waiting.

"Put two investigators on it. One for Zabini's Circus, one for Wilgilag. Time is of the essence," he said emphatically. "Reports within a week would be good."

"It will cost…" the solicitor began to warn.

"Irrelevant. Tell the guys to fax or phone me here. I want progress reports. Is that clear, Lionel?"

"Yes. Very clear. I'll get two top investigators to work immediately, giving your precise instructions."

"Thank you."

He was trying to get his thoughts in order for a call to Helen Carter at the head office of his travel agency when there was a knock on the library door.

Maggie, he thought, and his heart did a weird somersault and sent a buzz through his veins. Steady does

it, he sternly commanded. Wayward responses and
wrong reactions could do untold damage. Control had
to be maintained. Firm control.

First and foremost he had to establish goodwill and
push table-sharing at meals, get things back to normal,
do what his grandfather would have expected of him.
Courtesy was the key. Courtesy and control. Best to
stay right where he was, seated behind the desk and
looking at ease.

"Come in," he called, pitching his voice to a
bright, welcoming note.

Mrs Featherfield entered, carrying what looked like
a large ledger under her arm. "I hope I'm not interrupting anything important, Master Beau," she rushed
out, beaming a hopeful and eager smile at him.

He felt absurdly deflated, like having a prize
whipped away from him at the last moment. It made
him effusive in denial. "Not at all, Feathers. I always
have time for you."

"Oh! How nice!" She came forward with an air of
happy anticipation. "I wanted to show you my scrapbook."

Beau was surprised. "What have you been collecting?"

The book was placed on the desk in front of him.
"They're all the newspaper and magazine cuttings
about Mr. Vivian. I thought you might like to see
them. Especially the more recent ones, since you've
been away so long."

Beau opened the book and started leafing through.
"This is amazing! I had no idea you were keeping
such a record."

"Well, they are lovely memories, Master Beau.

Your grandfather was such a gentleman. Being in service to him was a real privilege.''

''I'm glad you felt that, Feathers,'' Beau said warmly.

''Indeed, I do. Nanny Stowe used to say he turned life into a rainbow.''

With a pot of gold at the end of it?

Or was it simply colour after rain?

Beau frowned as he recalled Maggie's claim of having led a very underprivileged life before coming to Rosecliff. *Without much to recommend her,* Sedgewick had said.

''Mr. Vivian loved having her with him,'' the housekeeper went on. ''And he was always determined she'd be the belle of the ball when he took her to those big charity dos.'' She leaned over the desk and turned a chunk of pages. ''Here they are!''

A photo of Maggie with his grandfather leapt out at him in full technicolour; his grandfather an elegant figure—as always—in a black dress suit and bow tie, turned admiringly towards a magnificent Maggie, wearing a stunning evening gown in black and burgundy, with exotic jet jewellery gleaming on her white skin and against her vivid hair.

''I remember that night well,'' Feathers said fondly. ''Mr. Vivian called us into the hall to watch her come down the staircase. He twirled his walking cane like a magician and called out, 'Hey, Presto!' and we clapped when she appeared. It was such fun! Mr. Vivian was delighted. He was so very, very proud of her.''

The scene described lingered in Beau's mind. He could see it quite vividly and it made poignant sense of all he had heard about the relationship between his grandfather and Maggie. It also made him feel mean-spirited for thinking badly of her. Of course, his grandfather had been the ringmaster. It was completely in character for him. As for Maggie...well, who would knock back the opportunity to be turned into a star?

"What was she like when she first came here, Feathers?"

"Nanny Stowe?"

"Yes." He turned to her with keen interest. "What impression did you have of her at the start...say, her first week at Rosecliff?"

No immediate answer...pensive...thinking back. When she spoke, the words came slowly. "It was like she'd been transported to another world and she couldn't quite believe it. Excited by the adventure but frightened of putting a foot wrong. And surprised. Mostly surprised."

"By what?" Beau prompted.

Feathers frowned. "I think...that we'd let her fit in here. I had the sense she wasn't used to belonging anywhere. What she brought with her...well, it was really pitiful. Some well-worn jeans and T-shirts, a couple of those cheap Indian dresses..." A shake of the head. "...The bare minimum of everything."

I tend to travel lightly.

"Of course, Mr. Vivian soon fixed that. I suggested she throw out her old clothes but she wouldn't." Another frown. "She said they were the only things that were hers."

The clothes Vivian bought me won't fit into my usual life.

"She had no idea how to make the most of herself, either. Seeing her now, you would hardly recognise her as the same girl who came here. No make-up, her glorious hair stuck into a plait. And she was thin. Too thin. All bones. Mr. Vivian said she was a thorough-bred racehorse who needed grooming and training. I remember how surprised she was when he showed her how she could look. Like she couldn't believe it was her."

Vivian is gone.

So was his magic wand, Beau thought. It's over for Maggie and she knows it.

You made me realise that today.

"She needed looking after," came the motherly opinion. "That's what I thought of her. She was like a waif of the world who'd never had anyone to look after her."

It's best I leave.

Beau was suddenly seized by a heart-squeezing suspicion. Maggie was gone. That was why she hadn't come down to breakfast. She had already left. Packed the things belonging to her and stepped back through the looking glass to the reality that had been hers before coming here.

He leapt up from his chair and barely quelled the impulse to go racing up to the Rose Suite. Her bedroom was off-limits for him. Absolutely. If she was there and he went banging on her door...it would be gross behaviour, open to distasteful interpretation.

"Is something wrong, Master Beau?"

The concern voiced by the housekeeper burrowed through his inner agitation. He looked at her distractedly, his mind dictating that any meeting with Maggie would have to be conducted on neutral ground.

"Feathers, I would like to talk to Nanny Stowe. Would you please go and ask her to join me here?"

"You mean...now?"

"Yes. Please."

"Shall I leave my scrapbook with you?"

"Yes. Thank you." He could barely curb his impatience. "It is rather urgent I see her," he pressed.

The housekeeper looked pleased. "I'll be as quick as I can, Master Beau."

She sailed off with an air of triumph. Beau was left with the strong impression she was in league with Sedgewick to *set him straight* on the subject of Nanny Stowe. However, neither of them could have any idea of what had transpired between him and Maggie last night. It complicated everything. There was no longer a simple line to take. Maggie may well have decided the game wasn't worth the candle if she had to take him into her life.

And if she had the missing million, why stay? Why put up with the aggravation of him when he couldn't get a damned thing right?

Beau paced around the library like a caged tiger. He'd messed up big-time, not giving Maggie Stowe the benefit of the doubt. He would have to chase after her if she'd gone. Which could present one hell of a problem. A woman from nowhere could easily slip back into nowhere, especially with a million untraceable dollars at her disposal.

He'd hate not knowing about the child, if there was to be one. To be left wondering would be a dreadful torture. It didn't matter that it hadn't been planned.

His child was his child. A fiercely paternal possessiveness swamped every other consideration and Beau
was on a feverish roll of resolution to pursue his
bloodline to the ends of the earth, if necessary, when
a knock on the door delivered a swift kick to his heart.

"Yes," he snapped, expecting bad news.

Maggie Stowe stepped into the library.

Disbelief choked Beau for a moment. The subsequent relief at seeing her was short-lived. She wore
jeans and a T-shirt and her gorgeous hair was confined
to a plait, making the contours of her face sharper and
the blue of her eyes more blue...guarded eyes, wary
and watchful as though he were a wild animal who
might strike at her, and she hugged the door, keeping
her escape route handy.

Beau's hand came up, a finger stabbing emphatically at her. "You are not to leave, Maggie."

Her chin came up. Defiance flared. "I don't believe
you have the right to tell me what to do, Mr.
Prescott."

"Oh, for God's sake, call me Beau! After what
we've shared, it's ridiculous to stick to formalities."

A flush stained her cheeks.

He was doing this wrong. Beau knew it but somehow couldn't stop it. Every time he saw her he went
haywire. "Relax! I'm not going to assault you," he
shot at her as he turned aside to walk to the desk and
put it between them. "Not that I did last night," he
added with a warning look over his shoulder. She was
not going to pin that on him. No way! He might be
guilty of a lot of things but he wasn't guilty of taking
an unwilling woman to bed with him.

"I have no intention of accusing you of anything, Mr. Prescott."

"Beau," he repeated with fierce insistence, glowering at her from behind the desk. "You are perfectly safe with me, I promise you. I just want to talk."

"Surely the simplest solution is for me to leave."

"No!"

"You could pretend this never happened. Out of sight, out of mind," she quietly argued.

"That won't work."

She looked bleakly at him. "What *will* work? You hate this. You're obviously upset. Why make a meal of it when I'm willing to walk away?"

"Is that what you were preparing to do? Without telling me?" Just the thought made him feel hollow inside.

"No. I agreed to wait until we know," she answered flatly.

"Why didn't you come down to breakfast?"

"I overslept."

"My grandfather wouldn't have bought those clothes for you," he pointed out.

"No. They are rightly mine." A flash of pride. "Vivian did pay me a salary and I bought some things for myself."

"Why are you wearing them?"

"I feel more comfortable in them."

"Because of me? Because of what I implied?"

She shrugged. "There's no reason to dress up anymore."

"I've spoilt it," he said regretfully.

"It doesn't matter."

"Yes, it does. I'm sorry. I really am."

She stared at him.

He could feel her scepticism and the turbulence of spirit behind it. He held her gaze, projecting sincerity, determined she know he genuinely rued the way he'd treated her. Whoever she was, whatever she was, she'd given something special to the last years of his grandfather's life and he did respect that.

"Please...I'd be grateful if you could overlook my manner to you regarding the clothes...and other things," he said, desperate to break the tension between them. "I've been very wrong to cast any aspersion on what gave everyone here pleasure. Most of all, my grandfather."

Her gaze slid away. Sadness was etched on her face. Beau wanted to reach out to her but didn't know how without seeming to be threatening. He searched his mind for a more effective peace-offering and couldn't come up with anything.

"I called a women's clinic." The soft words were directed at the carpet. It obviously took an act of will to bring her gaze up to his again and the resolution in her eyes didn't quite cover the fear and anguish behind it. "I can have a blood test in four days. It takes one working day for the results to be determined. A week all up, and we'll know one way or the other."

She didn't want to be pregnant. The realisation thumped into Beau's heart. He'd been wrong about that, too. Whatever had driven her response to him last night, it wasn't the possibility of having him father a child on her.

"They say a blood test is definitive," she added.

"I'll go with you," he said, impelled to stand by her and give what support he could.

Her mouth twisted. "Don't you trust me to do it right?"

He frowned, shook his head. "I just want to be there. Some people faint at having a blood test taken. You shouldn't be alone. I'm involved in this."

She looked at him quizzically, reassessingly, and Beau felt his pulse quicken with the hope he *was* getting through to her, touching a base that was more than physical.

Finally an ironic smile. "I guess it is a togetherness project. And it's best you are with me to make sure everything's correct. It removes all doubt."

Practical. The hope withered. She didn't trust him, didn't believe he would actually be concerned about her.

"If the test is positive, I *will* look after you, Maggie. And the child. I'll look after both of you," he declared emphatically.

Again she stared at him. He saw her throat move in a convulsive swallow. "It's my responsibility, too," she said huskily. "You don't have to feel...I don't want to be a loadstone around your neck. And there's nothing worse for a child than to feel... unwanted."

As she had been.

An abandoned baby.

"I promise you it won't be like that," he said with a fervour that rose so strongly in him Beau had to fight the impulse to cross the room and enfold her in a comforting embrace, promising her all the security he could provide.

''Well, if the test is negative, there won't be any problems,'' she said flatly.

Beau felt his whole body clench in rejection of that outcome. It was utter madness, he told himself. She was doing it to him again, getting under his skin, twisting him around, raising instincts that raged through him, robbing him of any common sense.

He wanted the child.

He wanted her.

And it didn't seem to matter that it made no sense at all.

Control and courtesy, his mind screamed, trying to hold on to the course of action he'd set himself. He took a deep breath, willing some oxygen into his brain.

''Maggie...could we start again?' His voice was hopelessly strained.

She looked blankly at him. ''Where?''

He tried to sort through the chaos she wrought in him and realised it was impossible to wipe the slate clean and pretend they were meeting for the first time.

''I'm sorry. I've given you every reason to think badly of me,'' he said in wretched disarray. ''I guess...what I want...is the chance to show I would be worth having around...if it comes to being parents.''

She eyed him thoughtfully. ''Yes. I would need to know that.''

''So, we have a truce?'' he pressed.

She slowly nodded.

Relief drained through him. He gestured his willingness to give. ''Is there anything I can do for you today?''

She shook her head, still wary of him, unsure where this was going. Beau cautioned himself against pushing too far.

"Well, I have some business with my travel agency so I'd better get on with it. I may go in to head office but I'll be back this evening. You'll join me for dinner?"

"If you like."

"Yes. And I'd feel better—everyone here would—if you'd wear whatever you'd normally wear for my grandfather. Please don't feel uncomfortable with it. I don't want to negate what he did."

She heaved a shaky sigh. "Are you sure about this, Beau? I don't like treading a minefield."

She'd called him Beau. He smiled, struggling to project reassurance rather than the sudden rush of exultation he felt. "I'm all out of bombs, Maggie."

The missing million could stay missing until further notice. He had other priorities right now.

"Well, I suppose a truce is a truce," she said without much conviction. "Tonight then," she said, a ghost of a smile on her lips. Having given the agreement, she slipped out of the library, closing the door quickly behind her.

It reminded Beau of leaving her suite last night.

Trapped.

The realisation struck. She was feeling it, too. With far more reason than he had! He wasn't the one who had to carry the pregnancy, give birth, bear all the burdens of becoming a mother.

He had to try to make this waiting time easier for her. It was the decent thing to do. Besides, he needed to score some positive points. Whether a baby eventuated or not, there was something about Maggie Stowe that got to him and he couldn't let her go. Not until he was...satisfied. Yes, satisfied. About everything.

himself in her, about some something about Maggie. Steve had got to him, and he couldn't let her go. Not until he was satisfied. Yes, asking. About everything.

CHAPTER TEN

MAGGIE felt miserably alone in her big bed, lying in the darkness, endlessly reviewing the past six days.

Playing with fire, she thought. Every time she was with Beau Prescott, it was playing with fire. And she was bound to get burnt.

It would have been better, safer, to have kept a solid distance from him since their night of madness which had so insidiously locked them into this waiting together. Instead, she had left the door open for him to infiltrate all her defences.

Just being with him put her at hazard, his physical presence playing havoc with her senses. The daily doses of charm and caring interest made her feel even more vulnerable, seeding hopes she knew had no solid basis for growing into something good.

If it all stopped tomorrow, if the test result was negative and he gave vent to any expression of "Thank God I'm saved!" Maggie knew she would shrivel up and die inside.

Yet if the test result was positive, how much weight could she attach to his turnaround in behaviour towards her? The paternal instinct might be aroused, but how long would it survive if resentment set in? *The wild child* might start chaffing against any tie. The will to be honourable could conflict very badly with the need to be free.

Maggie was acutely aware of his holding a rigid

control, especially over the simmering sexual attraction which neither of them admitted to on the surface. He didn't want to compound the problem they already had, didn't want to get so close there was no room for an easy retreat. The truce was simply a truce from which either of them could withdraw, no promises made, no obligations entered into. It was important to remember that when the deadline came tomorrow. She would hate to make a fool of herself.

The awful part was, no matter how complicated it made her future, she wanted to be pregnant with his child. Somehow—underneath all the conflicts between them—she still wanted to believe they were meant to mate. Surely when he had come to her, she had instinctively responded to that primitive urge. It was the only excuse she had for doing what she'd never done before... putting herself in jeopardy, in a position where there might be no way out.

The old fear suddenly seized her. She determinedly beat it away. There *was* a way out of this web of circumstances. She could simply step back into the life she'd had before coming here and leave all this behind.

She shifted restlessly, fervently wishing the long hours of this night were already over. Her bed offered no comfort. It kept evoking erotic memories, memories that made her feel a deep sensual craving for the same sexual experience to be repeated. Except she wanted the intimacies to be on more levels than the strictly physical. She was hopelessly obsessed with Beau Prescott, even though common sense dictated he was probably more her enemy than her friend.

Feeling torn by too many conflicting feelings,

Maggie tried to will herself to sleep. At least tomorrow would bring answers, whether she liked them or not. The doctor had promised the result would be telephoned and faxed through to them as soon as it came in, which would surely be tomorrow morning.

Answers were better than being in the dark.

Beau shifted restlessly in his bed. He'd used every relaxing technique he knew and they were all useless. His body knew damned well what it wanted—Maggie Stowe—and there was no telling it otherwise. Every night he craved to be in bed with her, wanting the wild heat of their coming together again. And every night he had to exercise this constant control over the torturous desires raging through him.

Thank God the truce would be over tomorrow. This limbo of waiting was killing him. After the result of the blood test came through he could move their relationship onto a different plane. If it was positive, surely the pregnancy would grant him the leeway to get closer to her. Closer in every sense. If it was negative, he would probably have to fight her decision to leave. Either way, it meant action…change…and he would have some barometer of what she was feeling towards him.

She couldn't deny there was a hell of a lot of chemistry between them. These things weren't one-sided and he had the evidence of that one night together to prove it. Nevertheless, he doubted sexual attraction was enough to hold her here.

This past week she had been very wary of him, certainly not inviting any touching. Even in conversation she'd been cautious, weighing her replies be-

fore giving them. It was obvious she didn't trust any
spontaneity with him, probably believing it had led
her astray and she wasn't about to repeat that mistake.
He suspected, in her mind, it was a huge mistake.

He now knew she usually shied clear of ties, never
staying long in one place, never attempting to put
down any roots. She frankly admitted to having been
a drifter, taking up an amazing array of jobs; crewing
on a yacht, picking tomatoes, waitressing, helping to
run camping tours, being a clown at children's parties.

She wouldn't be pinned down to when and where,
clearly suspicious of his motives for questioning her,
but the experiences she had related over these past
few days had a credibility he couldn't doubt. Besides
which, when he'd questioned Sir Roland about the
first meeting with his grandfather in the restaurant,
both accounts of the evening dovetailed. Maggie had
not lied nor embroidered the story in any way.

Having a string of godfathers did not fit what he
knew of her now. The missing million didn't fit,
either. She had a strong streak of independence and
an untouchable inner core which he equated with the
will of a survivor.

Remaining for two years at Rosecliff with his
grandfather was something exceptional in her life. He
was sure of that. But then the climate here had been
exceptional for her under his grandfather's rule…
acceptance without question, approval, liking, respect.
When those personal values were threatened she
moved on. At least, that was what had stood out to
him in the investigators' reports.

Beau knew those reports, word for word, having
read them so many times, endlessly analysing, trying

to solve the enigma of the woman from nowhere. Mrs. Zabini's statement still teased him with its implication of a harsh, subservient upbringing.

"I think she a runaway. No papers. Very few clothes. She say eighteen, but I think younger, maybe sixteen. Is difficult to get nanny to travel with circus so I not question too much. She say she come from big foster family and used to looking after little ones. Whether true or not, she very good with children. Do everything. No complaining.

"But not comfortable with people. Very shy. Keep to herself. I think she afraid of people. When police-men come round circus she hide. But she no thief. She never make trouble. I think she not want to be found. I think she run from bad things so I let be. The Zabinis know of running from bad things in old world. She not of old world, but fear is same.

"When we stop for our resting she leave. No want to stay in one place. My husband, he write reference for her. A good girl. Good nanny. She go with our blessing."

From Wilgilag, the story was much the same.

Very good with the children, but shied from adult company. Didn't talk about herself. No family. No connections. No mail ever came for her and she never wrote letters. Everything was smooth sailing—no problems, no trouble—until the owner's sister arrived for a visit. Her curiosity about the nanny, nagging her with questions, apparently drove the girl away. A cattletrain came in, loaded up, and she left with it. No goodbyes. No reference. Never heard anything more of her.

Beau wondered how long and how far Maggie had

kept running before she began to feel safe. The fear Mrs. Zabini had spoken of must have dissipated somewhere along the line before she'd met his grandfather or she wouldn't have been a participant in the publicity he invited. On the other hand, maybe she felt she looked so different, no one would identify her as the Margaret Stowe who had gone missing over ten years ago. She was also under the protection of a very wealthy man with influence in high places.

The situation had now changed and she could be getting ready to run again. Beau knew she didn't feel safe with him. The trick tomorrow would be to convince her she was. Especially if the test proved positive.

If it was negative...

Well, he wasn't really prepared for fatherhood. It hadn't been on his agenda. Having it thrust upon him was hardly ideal. Yet he knew he would be disappointed if a negative result came in.

Crazy...

As crazy as wanting Maggie Stowe so much, every cell in his body ached.

He didn't have the solution to anything.

He only knew that tomorrow had to move him closer to it.

CHAPTER ELEVEN

D-DAY, as Maggie thought of it, could not have been more sparkling. The morning was bathed in brilliant sunshine, the sky and harbour bright blue, not a cloud anywhere, no smear of city pollution. It could have been midsummer instead of autumn. It was the kind of day to make one say, ''God's in His heaven, all's right with the world.''

Except it wasn't all right for Maggie.

She tried to brighten herself up by wearing yellow. When she went down to breakfast, Beau was already at the table, perusing a newspaper. Sedgewick was refilling his glass with orange juice. The ''Good mornings'' exchanged rang with good cheer, sincerely so on Sedgewick's part.

Beau looked tired around the eyes, as though he hadn't slept any better than she had. The strain of this entrapped situation was beginning to show, Maggie thought, her heart sinking even lower at the prospect of the news to come...the news which would almost certainly blast this beautiful day and bring the winds of change.

''Jeffrey is preparing a special treat this morning,'' Sedgewick informed them as he poured her a glass of juice.

Maggie's stomach hosted so many butterflies she didn't feel like eating anything.

"He is an exceptionally good chef," Beau remarked.

And well he might, Maggie thought, considering the stream of *treats* that had been coming from the kitchen all week. In Sedgewick's opinion, good food promoted good humour and the butler was leaving no stone unturned in encouraging what he now saw as a promising relationship. Jeffrey undoubtedly had orders to soothe with excellence and titillate with innovation.

"He considers himself an artist, Master Beau," Sedgewick answered, beaming benevolent approval at the reformed *wild child.*

"So what gourmet delight is he producing this morning?" Beau asked with a show of eager interest.

Was it forced? Maggie wondered. How could his stomach not be in knots? Was he confident of taking *any outcome* in his stride?

"Jeffrey has a friend, sir, who comes from Louisiana. I understand the dish is a favourite there. Fried green tomatoes. Quite delectable, sir. I have sampled it. I promise you are sure to enjoy it."

"*Green* tomatoes?" Maggie questioned.

"Yes, indeed. Slices of them coated in a golden crust which has a subtle taste of garlic and onion."

Garlic was the last thing Maggie needed this morning.

"Tell Jeffrey we await the pleasure," Beau said, apparently relishing a new eating experience. His eyes were twinkling, despite the look of fatigue on his face. His happy air of anticipation was absolutely incomprehensible to Maggie.

Sedgewick served her with her usual fruit compote

and sailed off to the kitchen to deliver the good news. She picked up her spoon and stared at the fruit—slices of peach, pear and mango. Easy enough to slide down, she thought. Maybe she should leave them until after the fried green tomatoes. They might kill the aftertaste of garlic and settle any queeziness in her stomach.

"That yellow dress looks wonderful on you, Maggie," Beau said warmly. "I must say it's very heart-lifting to see."

The compliment startled her. She looked at him, wondering what he meant by it.

He offered an appealing smile. "I do hope it means I'm forgiven for my trespasses."

Her mind remained blank, unable to find any connection to what he was saying.

"I was sitting here, dreading the possibility you might appear in your jeans, ready for a quick take off," he explained.

Finally it clicked. He was thinking of their meeting in the library, the morning after...when she'd offered to leave then and there, only agreeing to stay until the results were known and they were clear of the pregnancy fear.

"You don't want me to go...no matter what?' she tested, wary of taking anything for granted with him.

"Absolutely not," he answered firmly.

Her heart hopped, skipped and jumped. His niceness to her over this past week couldn't have been a pretence. Why would he invite a longer pretence than he had to? Maybe he really had begun to like her as a person. Or...maybe he was still feeling guilty about not treating her as his grandfather would have wanted, still doing penance for his *trespasses*.

Before she could form a question that might ascertain his motives, Mr. Polly intruded, carrying in a basket of roses, his weather-beaten face wreathed in pleasure.

"Please excuse me, Master Beau…"

"Of course, Mr. Polly."

"…Prize blooms, these are. I told Mr. Vivian they would be this year. He said to enter them in the Royal Easter Show if they came out this good."

"Well, go right ahead and do it," Beau encouraged. "They look like winners to me."

"Double Delight," Mr. Polly almost crooned as he held one up for them to admire. "That's what they're called. Because of the red and white in the petals."

"What a perfect rose!" Maggie exclaimed.

"Perfect for you, Nanny Stowe. I thought you might like these for your room."

He was such a sweetie. "How kind! They're so beautiful!" she said warmly.

"I'll take them to Mrs. Featherfield to put them in water for you. And may I say, you've always been a Double Delight, Nanny Stowe." He looked meaningly at Beau. "I felt sure you would see a prize in them, sir. Thank you for your permission to put an entry in the show."

Maggie felt herself colouring red on white as the head gardener took his leave of them, having delivered a remark which had the subtlety of a sledgehammer. She quickly picked up her spoon and delved into the fruit compote, hoping Beau was oblivious to her being labelled as a prize worth recognising. To her, the whole staff were embarrassingly obvious with wanting *the chance* for their relationship to develop into a happy-ever-after and secure future for everyone.

"You see? My life here wouldn't be worth living if you left, Maggie," Beau said in dry amusement.

Reluctantly she met his gaze and he grinned at her as he expounded on the situation. "Sedgewick would order Jeffrey to dish up slops for each meal. I'd be sent to coventry by Mrs. Featherfield. Wallace would undoubtedly ensure the grumpiest, bumpiest ride in the Rolls. And Mr. Polly would grow thorns."

She couldn't grin back. It wasn't funny. "They've been with your grandfather a long time, Beau," she reminded him. "They're frightened of change. You should understand that before deciding on whatever course you'll take."

He weighed her words. "You care about them."

"They've all contributed to giving me the best part of my life. Of course, I care about them. They're good people. With the kindest of hearts."

"All the more reason for you to stay on then."

Maggie wasn't sure of that. It could be prolonging hopes that were better cut dead so they didn't obscure the realities to be faced.

"We'll see," she said noncommittally.

The reasons Beau was giving were centred on him—his comfort—not on any feelings for her. The hope that had danced through her bloodstream a few minutes ago, fell limply by the wayside. She ate the fruit without thinking about it, without even tasting it.

Sedgewick returned. The fried green tomatoes were served. Beau was suitably complimentary about the Louisiana dish. Maggie made agreeable murmurs and washed the glug in her mouth down with coffee. Nothing more of any importance was said.

After breakfast, Maggie excused herself to see to the roses Mr. Polly had left with Mrs. Featherfield.

"I'll be in the library," Beau said pointedly.

Where the fax machine was, Maggie thought, and found herself trembling. She clenched her hands, stiffened her spine and sternly told herself she would cope with everything better once she knew the test result.

In the end, she didn't join Beau in the library, waiting for the news. She simply couldn't bear to be with him. Having arranged the perfect Double Delight blooms in a vase, she carried it up to her suite, placed it on her dressing table, then wandered around the bedroom that had once seemed like a place fit for a princess.

It still was, but it no longer made her feel like a princess. The rosewood antique furniture was beautiful, gleaming with a perfect polish and set off with ornate brass handles. The pink silk canopy above the bed was splendidly draped, adding its richness to the rose print bedspread. Deeply sashed pink curtains dressed the French doors, falling into luxurious pools on a floor thickly carpeted in the palest of green. She loved it all. She had been very happy here. Yet now she felt outside it.

She stopped in front of the cheval mirror and stared at her reflection. Vivian's re-imaged Maggie Stowe looked back at her. Strange how the outer shell could almost make one believe the inner self had been changed, too, but it wasn't really so. Right now this image superimposed a lot of other Maggie Stowes but they still existed in her heart.

There was the unpolished, uncultured young woman Vivian had met. Maggie could still see her peering through the added gloss and style...a streetwise survivor who'd learnt most of the games people played and how to duck or slide past them. Life wasn't easy without paper qualifications. Exploitation was not uncommon in the casual job market, especially when the employee had no family to back her up and no easy recourse to the law. Maggie never let herself get caught in webs like that. Just a touch of it and she moved on.

The mirror shimmered as her vision reached further into the past...to the fear-filled girl/woman who'd found safe refuge with Zabini's Circus as she struggled to come to terms with a world teeming with all sorts of different people and different places and different ways of life. Impossible to have envisaged what she'd meet once she left the restricted world of the compound.

Her mind flicked at the suppressed memories of that earlier life...the discipline, the subservience, the constant demand to respect the good teachings, the secret growth of resistance, rebellion, and the need to keep it hidden until she was old enough, grown up enough to escape.

You with the red curls, cast your eyes down, girl!

Maggie saw herself at six, a thin child, all eyes and hair. She couldn't hide her hair. Confining it in a plait had made it less obvious. But she'd learnt the lesson of casting her eyes down because it hid her thoughts and feelings.

She'd learnt the wisdom in the kind advice from her first housemother who had probably recognised a rebellious spirit…best to bow the head, best to obey, best to keep in line, best not to bring any notice to herself. That way she could live in her mind, in the dream worlds she kept to herself.

She couldn't remember when she'd begun to believe there had to be a bigger, better life outside the compound. The fence was to keep them protected from bad things, they were told. But the grown-ups came and went. They didn't seem to mind going out there to whatever existed beyond the fence. When she was grown up enough she would go and find out for herself.

And she had.

Then she knew the fence hadn't been about protection at all. It had been about power. And the compound had been a prison, although supposedly a benevolent one. She'd never let anything become a prison again. The sense of anything closing in on her set nerves jangling. Freedom had become an important value in her life. Or maybe it always had been…something genetic that not even the commune discipline could crush out of her.

Where had these genes come from? If her mother and father had ever lived in the compound, she'd never recognised them and they'd never acknowledged her. None of the grown-ups she'd seen had red hair, although she realised that was not conclusive. Who were they…the man and woman who had created the person she was?

The mirror didn't give up those answers.

They were forever lost to Maggie.

Her mind slowly swam up through the layers of the past, back to the reflection in front of her…Vivian's sculpture from the material she'd been, the material she still was within the different shaping. It had been Vivian who had held her together like this. Without him…it was getting harder to hold on to it, to keep believing it was real.

The faithful four—Sedgewick, Mrs. Featherfield, Wallace, Mr. Polly—were trying to hold on to it, but it wasn't the same without Vivian. Beau didn't believe in her. That was the crux of it. He didn't see what his grandfather had seen and Vivian's Maggie Stowe was beginning to lose her reality.

She moved away from the mirror and sat down on the edge of the bed, wrapped in a sense of hiatus as she waited for the news which would form decisions and directions for her. Eventually a knock came on the door and Beau called out to her. His voice echoed through her head, forcing a set of instructions to form.

Get up.

She pushed herself onto her feet.

Go and open the door to him.

Her legs were shaky. She felt sick, dizzy. The news he was bringing to her carried such enormous import. She sat down again, trembling.

Another knock. Another call. It had to be answered. She took a deep breath, trying to ease the fierce grip of tension. Words still had to be forced.

"Come in."

The old training suddenly slid out and took over. She sat very still, her fingers interlaced on her lap, head bent, eyes cast down, mental shield up. No one could get at her that way. She could take in what she needed to and leave out the rest.

She heard Beau come in and close the door behind

him. It didn't occur to her it might be inappropriate to invite him into her bedroom. In her mind she wasn't really anywhere…just waiting.

He didn't say anything. She felt his eyes on her, scrutinising, assessing, felt his approach, the energy of him coming closer and closer, saw his feet, pressing into the thick carpet in front of her. He held out a sheet of fax paper for her to read. It took several moments for her to focus her eyes on the typewritten message.

The test result was positive.

CHAPTER TWELVE

BEAU could feel his heart thumping wildly as he
waited for a reaction. The printed result had to snap
Maggie out of whatever far place she had retreated
to. He wanted to speak to her, yet his mind was such
a jumble of thoughts and concerns, he was riven with
uncertainty over what to say. Fact—proven fact—had
a shattering effect on preconceived suppositions and
her withdrawal from him wasn't helping to put anything sensible together.

He'd stepped into this room with a sense of honourable purpose. The seemingly frozen image of her,
sitting in a pose of passive submission, had instantly
unsettled him. There was something terribly wrong
about it. The vibrant vitality he associated with her
wasn't simply guarded. It had receded. He felt as
though he was looking at an uninhabited shell.

The urge to pick her up and shake life back into
her was almost irresistible. His mind cautioned that
any touching might trigger an extremely adverse response. His body desperately wanted to heat hers to
a sizzling awareness of what they had shared while
creating the result he now held out to her.

"I think we should get married, Maggie."

Her head jerked up, her vivid blue eyes wide and
whirling with shock.

Beau was shocked, too. It wasn't what he had
planned to say. He didn't know where the words had

come from. They'd spilled off his lips before he could think better of them.

"No!" She leapt up, suddenly, explosively invigorated, colour shooting into her face, a bright flash of recoil in her eyes as she palmed him aside in her agitated move away from him. "No!" Her head shook in vehement denial. She walked in an erratic course around the room. "No, I can't! I can't!" she cried, then made a beeline for the French doors, clearly driven towards escape.

"Why not?" Beau demanded aggressively, any common sense completely smashed by her extreme reaction. Never mind that he'd only meant to suggest marriage as a possibility to consider. Wasn't he one of the most eligible bachelors around? He was in a position to virtually offer her the world on a silver platter. Why the hell wasn't she seeing that and evaluating the advantages?

She paused, her hands curled around the knobs of the doors. She didn't turn back to him. Her shoulders heaved. Tension screamed from her. "It would be...*a prison*," she said, the dark revulsion in her voice slicing straight into his heart.

A prison? Beau was stunned speechless. The concept of marriage to him being a prison was horrifying enough, but the way she'd said it...as though it would be an unbearable torture!

The doors were opened and she was out on the balcony before he could raise a protest. Escaping from him, as though his offer had conjured up something monstrous. Beau's insides twisted into knots. This wasn't right. It was no more right than the way she had been sitting when he'd come in.

He stared down at the paper in his hand. Maggie Stowe was pregnant with *his* child. Whatever was disturbing her so deeply had to be resolved. He couldn't let her move on from him, dropping out of sight and out of contact. His whole being revolted against that eventuality. He had to reach out to her, into her, and somehow hold her to him.

Pumped up to fight for the outcome he wanted, Beau tossed the fax sheet on the bed and followed her out to the balcony. She was standing against the balustrade, as far away from him as she could get. Her gaze was aimed at the far north shore of the harbour, above and beyond the artfully landscaped gardens of Rosecliff, as though her immediate surroundings—however beautiful—were part and parcel of what she needed to get away from.

"How can you call Rosecliff a prison?"

The question shot from his mouth as he stepped up to the balustrade, turning to scrutinise her profile and discern whatever he could from her expression. He had to start with something and hopefully she'd give him enough signals to find a path to an understanding between them.

She rigidly ignored him. Or rigidly held herself in.

"You could have all this..." He waved at the grounds below them, property that would be coveted by anyone. "...If you married me."

She closed her eyes. Her fingers curled more tightly over the curved top of the balustrade. Her body wavered slightly. Beau waited, not prepared to rush into any judgment. He'd already made too many mistakes with Maggie Stowe.

"It's people who make a prison, not a property,"

she answered, as though dragging the words from some deep place inside her.

People? What people?

She turned her head and looked at him, her eyes burning with unshakable conviction and an accusation that reduced his material argument to ashes in the wind. "It's the people in charge of the compound. The people in power. They make the prison."

Him? How could she equate him with a prison?

He stared at the searing knowledge in her eyes and his stomach curled. This wasn't some theoretical philosophy. She had lived through what she was saying and it was still very real to her, traumatically real. He'd wanted to learn what drove Maggie Stowe and here it was...an experience so soul-scarring she couldn't move past it, not even with all the running she'd done over the years.

She turned her gaze back to the far horizon. "I won't live like that," she said with fierce determination. "I won't let my child be subjected to it. I'll keep us both safe. And *free*."

Her voice shook with the emphasis she gave to freedom. Beau found himself intensely moved by it. He understood the desire for freedom, empathised with it, but he knew intuitively this was more than desire. It was need...deep-rooted need.

His mind flicked to Mrs. Zabini's statement. Not a runaway, he thought, an escapee from a prison. Though it couldn't have been a government institution...nothing criminal. The investigators hired by Lionel Armstrong would have turned up any official records of her. Maybe the prison had been some private orphanage. A big foster family, she'd told Mrs.

Zabini. Yet surely those also came under the jurisdiction of the social welfare arm of government.

She'd used the word, *compound*. Beau had an instant vision of high, secure fences. Illegal immigrants were kept in a compound until their cases could be evaluated. But once again, that was government business. How had Maggie remained outside the official net until she was—Mrs. Zabini's guess—sixteen?

Whatever the answer, that wasn't his immediate problem and he doubted she'd tell him anyway. She was equating him with *the people in charge, the people in power*. He had to change that view of him and do it convincingly or she would disappear from his life. The issue was not material advantages to her.

Acceptance, approval, liking, respect...those values overrode everything else in Maggie Stowe's mind. That was decisively brought home to him now. If he couldn't answer them...

He took a deep breath. The sense of being on the edge of a precipice was very strong. One careless step and he was gone. He'd wanted action with Maggie...any action. He'd had no idea the ground was so perilous.

A trapped animal will always turn on its captor, he thought. He had to soothe, win her trust, move them both back to a safe place where they could negotiate with each other.

"Why do you see marriage to me as a prison, Maggie?' he asked quietly, careful to keep any judgmental note out of his voice.

She shivered. "You're only thinking of what you want, Beau."

It was a flat statement, uncoloured by the emotions

he suspected were still ripping through her. The truth of it was undeniable.

"I want what would be best for all three of us, Maggie, not only myself," he countered softly.

"I haven't given you the right to judge what's best for me. And I'll fight you over judging for my child, as well." She turned to him, eyes blazing in challenge. "No one will ever take from me the right to be my own person and make my own judgments."

He frowned. "I'm sorry. I didn't mean to do that."

"Yes, you did. Why else would you want marriage if not to lock me and our child into your life where you'll be in legal charge of us?"

"I just wanted to be in a position where I could take care of both of you," he argued, sincere in this belief of himself.

"You wouldn't respect my wishes. You don't care about my feelings."

Another flat statement. He struggled against it. He did care. He felt a tumult of caring right now. But he could see she wouldn't believe it. "I have tried to show you differently this past week," he said, searching for some way to appease the hurt he'd given.

She shook her head. There was a twist of irony on her lips as she answered, "There's a difference between being civilised and actually accepting a person in your heart. Liking them. Wishing them well. You think I don't know it?"

He'd done his best to stand back from the attraction he felt, seeking the truth about her. He hadn't wanted to be any more stupid than he had been. But he couldn't offer those reasons as excuses for his manner towards her.

Her eyes mocked his dilemma. "From the very start you didn't trust me, Beau. You still don't. That's why you want to lock me in."

It was terribly disconcerting that she saw him so clearly, saw what he himself hadn't quite grasped until she laid it out to him. She shamed him with her truths. All his actions had been motivated by what *he* wanted while she had been the hub of endlessly rotating wheels of suspicion.

"Maggie, is the pregnancy a prison? I mean...not thinking about its tie to me. Apart from that..." He hated asking this question but he had to, in fairness to her, aware that *he* had driven the course to these consequences and wanting to remove the trapped feeling she had to have. "...Do you want to have the child?"

"Yes. Yes, I do," she answered decisively, without even a slight hesitation.

Beau breathed a huge sigh of relief. "So do I."

She slanted him a look, checking if he meant it.

He tried an appealing smile. "I know it's not the most propitious circumstances, Maggie, but I can't help feeling excited about it."

She frowned. "You don't mind about me being the mother?"

"I can't imagine anyone better."

It bewildered her. "But you don't like me."

With a devastating jolt, Beau realised this was the crux of her flight from his proposal of marriage. Without liking, there couldn't be respect or approval or acceptance. Her logic could not be faulted. And he *was* guilty of doubting her fitness as the mother of his child. But he'd learnt so much more about her since then.

"That's not true, Maggie," he said with passionate insistence. "You blew my mind the day I arrived home and I've been struggling to get it together ever since. I now believe a woman who could make my discerning grandfather so happy and so proud of her, is a woman well worth knowing. And I believe a woman who inspires so much caring from our live-in staff has to have a very caring heart herself."

He saw her face tightening, felt her resistance to what he was saying, and in sheer desperation, cried, "Maggie, I swear to you, I no longer see in you anything not to like."

He knew, the moment the words were out, he'd emphasised a negative instead of a positive. He saw the recoil in her eyes, the bleak dismissal of this line of pursuit even before she spoke.

"I guess it suits you to say such things, now that I have something you want."

It was a judgment he deserved, but it hurt. The rejection of his earnest endeavours to alter her impression of him hurt, too. He realised he'd delivered too many hurts himself, striking at vulnerabilities he hadn't known existed, hadn't stopped to look for them behind his grandfather's *creation*.

Blinded by prejudice.

Too many prejudices.

Where was his salvation now?

Despair dragged at his determination. He'd dug his own grave and made the walls too high for him to climb out of it. Or maybe he was using the wrong approach. He had to keep trying, no matter what.

"What do you want to do, Maggie?" he asked, humbled by her painfully accurate reading of the situation. "What would make you feel…right?"

CHAPTER THIRTEEN

MAGGIE didn't know what would make her feel right. She didn't know what to do. She lifted her gaze to a sky so endlessly blue it seemed to stretch on to infinity. Her heart ached with so many griefs, her mind couldn't encompass them all. They slid into a desperate, silent plea for help.

Vivian...Vivian...

Where was he? Did he see it had gone terribly wrong? It was such wicked, painful irony...the marriage he'd wanted between her and Beau...the child to carry on his family line...it was in her power to deliver on the promise...yet her soul revolted against accepting the form it was taking.

Give it a chance...

I did. I tried. It can't work like this, she cried, exonerating herself from the burden laid on her.

Yet the needs of others kept pulling her back to it, denying her release.

Sedgewick... *You must cultivate a positive attitude.* Was she being too negative in the face of Beau's desire to keep her and the child?

Mrs. Featherfield... *A new baby at Rosecliff. I can't imagine anything more perfect.* Was it fair to deprive her child of its natural inheritance?

Wallace seeing sexual attraction as the answer...and she couldn't deny it had led to this shared parenthood. Given more open expression, might it not

139

bridge this dreadful gap between them and soften their differences?

Mr. Polly... *Nature will take its course. A little help and care and you can always get the result you want.*

Could Beau learn to care?

Did a baby help?

Would anything change if she gave it more of a chance, or would the prison gates inexorably close her in if she stayed on here?

She took a deep breath and looked at him...this man who knew her intimately yet did not know her at all. Vivian's grandson. The father of her child.

Her heart fluttered at that last thought. It was real now. The father of her child. She couldn't deny him, yet...what would it lead to?

"How can I trust you?" she blurted out, anguished by her uncertainties.

A muscle in his cheek contracted but his eyes didn't waver from hers, dark pools of green, seemingly reflecting the pain she felt. "It would need you to take a risk, Maggie," he said quietly. "I can't prove your trust is not misplaced unless you're willing to chance it."

"Marriage is too big a risk for me, Beau."

He nodded, then managed a wry smile. "A classic case of fools rushing in... I'm sorry, Maggie. My understanding has been very amiss. I seem to have blundered all the way along the line with you and I wish like hell I'd done everything differently. But I know that doesn't make anything better for you."

His regretful attitude soothed some of her jangling nerves. He probably thought she was mad, rejecting his offer of marriage out of hand, and so fiercely.

Impossible to explain just how threatened she'd felt at that moment, with him looming over her in a pose of commanding authority and the bank of distrust forming too dangerous a current for her to ride.

He looked…almost kind now. Caring. Of course, it could be another pose. On the other hand, there had to be good in him. Everyone at Rosecliff couldn't be entirely deceived on that point. Maybe with their child, he would show his best side. He couldn't hang anything nasty on an innocent baby.

What was it about her that brought out the mean judgments he made? If they were to be linked by their child, she needed to understand where he was coming from with her. At least that way she would be more prepared for handling the situation. She searched for some meeting ground and instinctively homed in on the person who'd brought them together.

"Vivian loved you, Beau. Very much."

"I know," he murmured encouragingly.

"He expected…because we were both dear to him…he wanted us to like each other."

"Yes, he would," came the ready agreement.

"I warned him it might not happen. I was always prepared to leave if you didn't like me. After all, you were his grandson. His real family. I thought you might see me as a usurper of his affections…"

"Maggie, I don't see you like that," he quickly assured her. "Nothing and no one could have changed the bond between my grandfather and me. It was unique to us. Just as I'm sure what you shared with him was unique to you."

Yes it was. Wonderfully, unbelievably unique. No one could ever guess, ever comprehend what it had meant to her. Which was why she had to be as fair as it was reasonably possible to Vivian's grandson.

"You could have been jealous," she suggested, still unsure of his feelings where she was concerned.

"No. Not in any possessive way, Maggie. My grandfather gave of himself to many people. It never diminished what he gave to me."

He sounded so genuine, so reasonable, it made no sense of what he'd done. "Then why have you been so mean to me?" she bluntly asked, searching his eyes for the true answer.

He grimaced, guilt and shame flicking over his face. "I was upset over not having seen my grandfather for so long. I guess I felt cheated by his dying when he did. And when I first arrived home you did seem like a usurper, acting the mistress of the house, the staff taking their lead from you. I simply wasn't prepared for what I walked into, Maggie, and it chewed me up. I'm sorry you became a target of distrust."

A target...the focus of all his bad feelings. Yes, she could accept that explanation. But it didn't make her feel any safer with him.

"You aren't anymore, Maggie," he assured her, an earnest plea for forgiveness in his eyes. "I realise they're probably empty words to you but they're true."

She wished she could believe them. "Vivian asked me...he made me promise...to give it a chance. Liking you, I mean. Being open to liking. He knew...understood...I tend to be wary of people."

"I wish he'd still been here to say the same to me," Beau said ruefully. "It would have been different,

Maggie. I am genuinely sorry for all the misunderstandings."

"I'm sorry, too. Because I don't trust you now, Beau. I'd leave here today except…it's Vivian's grandchild and I know I wouldn't feel right, not giving it every chance to work out something we can live with…amicably."

"Then may I make a suggestion?"

She nodded, having no ready answers in her own mind.

"Come away with me for a while. People get to know each other very well when travelling together. I want to scout a tour through Europe so it'll be a business trip for me." He suddenly grinned, a sparkle of gentle teasing in his eyes. "You can accompany me as my nanny, if you like, looking after the kind of things you did for my grandfather."

Laughter bubbled out of her throat. Maybe it was the absurdity of the idea or some form of hysterical relief from nervous tension. Maggie shook her head, feeling too limp and drained to care.

"No pressures, I promise you," Beau went on, his voice eager with the wish to persuade. "Separate rooms. And you'll have your ticket home so you can leave me anytime you choose."

A trip to Europe…fantasy, she thought, but a very seductive one. Vivian had always been referring to places there.

"It's a break away from here, Maggie. It'll make it easier for you to leave Rosecliff, if you must. You won't be upsetting Sedgewick and the others. I think they'd all approve of me taking you with me."

He was right about that, she thought ironically, though it couldn't really be done.

"And I will look after you, Maggie," Beau pressed. "If you'll risk the chance to let me show you, it's a step towards resolving the future, isn't it?"

He looked so keen. Her heart jiggled painfully. "It's...it's a good suggestion, Beau. I'd like to try it...but...it just isn't possible."

He frowned. "Why not?"

She flushed at the hopelessness of a situation he probably couldn't comprehend. "Apart from the bank account Vivian organised for me with his accountant, for my salary to be paid into, I have nothing to prove who or what I am. Vivian and Mr. Neville were referees for me to the bank manager because I didn't have any of the usual forms of identification. But that won't do for a passport."

"You have your birth certificate..."

"No. I don't. I tried to get a copy once but the registry wanted information I didn't know," she confessed. "And it's no use looking for the answers. No one would admit anything now. I may not have even been registered."

She turned her gaze out to the harbour, once more awash with the helpless feeling of a dislocated person with no roots and nothing to steer by. I'm like a piece of flotsam on the water, she thought, but at least I'm still afloat. Better than being submerged in hopelessness.

"Maggie, let me help you with this. There must be people who know..."

She shook her head. "You don't understand, Beau.

It's not there anymore. They've gone. If there were records, they've gone, too.''

"What's not there, Maggie?'' he asked quietly.

She'd said too much. It was really better not to say anything. People didn't—couldn't—relate to something so far outside their experience. She remembered telling a workmate once. It made the woman look at her differently, as though she were some kind of freak.

"Are you afraid of...whatever's gone?'' It was a soft, tentative question, sensitive to her feelings.

She had no reason to be anymore. No one could take her back to that life in the compound. She'd been free of that fear for many years, but the sense of having a big chunk of her life stolen and used for the supposedly higher purposes of others never left her.

"Maggie...will you trust me with this? You can stand on judgment of me right now. I want to help, to move forward with you.''

She heard the plea in his voice and it touched her. The father of my child, she thought. Was it right to drop the shield with him? If she did, would they move forward or would he back off?

Best to know.

"All right.''

She shifted to the corner of the balcony, instinctively putting distance between them before she turned to face him. A challenge like this required space. He stood side on to the balustrade, watching her, waiting, maintaining an air of confidence that encouraged her to unburden herself on him.

Maggie put the past at a distance, too. It was easier to pretend it had happened to someone else, a part of her that she was now separated from, a different person. She knew it wasn't really true but the disconnection allowed her to speak more objectively.

"I was brought up in a kind of commune. There were about fifty children. Different ages. Eight to a house with a housemother in charge. None of us knew who our real parents were or if we had any at all. None of us had any memory of a life outside the compound."

He didn't show any shock at all. "You were always kept inside it?" he asked, gently inquisitive.

"Yes. The idea was...we were the innocent children of God and we were to be kept pure from the world. It was a cult thing. I guess you could call it a social experiment."

His face tightened but he nodded for her to go on.

"We were taught to read and write but had no formal schooling or examinations as I later discovered the children outside took for granted. Music was a big part of our daily routine, singing and playing hymns and good songs. If you didn't question anything, it wasn't a bad life. Very regimented, very disciplined, very...stifling."

"It was a prison to you," he said softly.

She winced, aware of having given that away too tellingly to refute. "There was no freedom...for anything. No privacy except in your own mind. I escaped when I was fourteen."

He looked surprised. "That young?"

"I was tall. I could pass for older."

"Where was the compound, Maggie?"

"Northwest New South Wales. Deep country. It's been abandoned."

"How long ago?"

"Eight years. I was twenty when the news of its existence broke. I don't know who or what tipped off government officials but the compound was raided and the children were taken away and put in the hands of welfare people to sort out. Those who were in charge of the compound—they were called The Inner Circle—destroyed whatever records they'd kept and skipped the country."

"They weren't pursued?"

"Traced to Hawaii, but they disappeared from there. There was a flurry of investigative journalism. More sensational than helpful. Problems with the children being assimilated into normal society. The older ones found it most difficult, wanting to go back to the safety of the compound."

"You didn't think of coming forward at that time and telling your story?"

"It came out in the newspaper stories that there were professional people—doctors and lawyers—who'd helped the Inner Circle get children who were given up for adoption. Abandoned babies. I didn't trust the people in power. I didn't know what they might do to me. Besides, I was making my own way. I didn't want what they might think of as help."

"Fair enough." No criticism. He seemed to understand the dilemma she'd faced. "Did you tell my grandfather any of this, Maggie?"

"Yes. But not for a long time. It's hardly a subject I care to bring up. To begin with, when he wanted to know my bank account, which I didn't have, I just told him I'd always worked for cash in hand and most of that went in day-to-day living." She shrugged. "It was the truth. There was no other way to avoid the paperwork I had no answers for.''

''He didn't press you about your lack of official status?''

''Why should he? The accountant made me official enough to cover Vivian's requirements. The question of a passport never came up.''

''I see,'' Beau murmured, then looked at her quizzically. ''When did you tell him what you've just told me?''

She paused for thought. ''He was talking about family lines. He wanted to know my...my background. It would have been about two months before he died.''

Beau heaved a sigh that seemed to hold both relief and satisfaction. ''Thank you for confiding in me. It answers a lot.''

Maggie didn't want to ask what it answered. If he was now seeing her in a different light, it didn't show. It didn't seem to be affecting him one way or another.

''Will you come with me to Europe, Maggie?' he asked.

''I told you...''

''I'll get you a passport. I'll get you all the official identification you'll need for anything, whether you come with me or not.''

''But how?''

''Believe me, I have the power and the resources to do it.''

She stared at the resolution stamped on his face and felt something hard and cold inside her start to warm and melt. ''You'd do that for me?'' Her voice was a bare whisper.

"Yes. I'll put it in motion at once."

Decisive, confident, fearless. Maggie was sharply reminded of her first impression of him...the aggressive vitality of the man, the flow of positive energy, the innate power that seemed to proclaim he could overcome anything or anyone, a hunter who always succeeded in attaining his goal, no matter what road he had to take or what hardship he had to endure.

A mate worth having...fighting for her...

She felt the stirring of desire again, the pins and needles of promising possibilities. Hope danced in and out of her brain, taunting her caution, fraying her doubts. He was waiting on her answer to the suggestion he'd made. Not forcing. Waiting for her to choose, of her own free will. Her heart insistently pumped one message...give it a chance.

"Then I will," she said huskily. "I will come with you to Europe." She managed a wobbly smile. "As a nanny."

CHAPTER FOURTEEN

"THIS is so exciting!" Mrs. Featherfield bubbled, her eyes darting around the Rose Suite to check for any item that might have been overlooked. "Are you sure you have everything packed?"

"The list has all been ticked off," Maggie assured her, almost light-headed with the enormity of the step she was about to take. "And I put it in the lid of the suitcase as you told me so I won't leave anything behind."

The housekeeper's smile beamed with pleasure and self-satisfaction. "I taught Master Beau that a long time ago." Tears suddenly welled into her eyes. "I remember when Mr. Vivian took him off to Europe. I'm sure Mr. Vivian would be delighted this has come about with you, my dear."

Maggie gave her a quick hug, barely containing her own flood of emotion. "It was good of Beau to think of it," she said huskily.

"He has a generous heart. Just like his grandfather. You'll be safe with him, dear."

Maggie was beginning to believe it. He'd been so different to her these past four weeks, treating her as an equal, caring, considerate, including her in planning the itinerary so she could read about the places and have the pleasure of anticipation, answering all her questions with good-natured patience and obvious enjoyment.

Best of all, he'd done what he said he'd do.
Amazingly, she now had a birth certificate, credit
cards and a passport, which made her feel like a real
person. Even though there were no names of a mother
and father on her birth certificate, it hadn't been a
deep disappointment. Somehow she'd accepted having no parents a long time ago. It was better not to
have them, knowing they'd cared so little for her
they'd abandoned her to the unknown…a foundling.

Besides, it was more than heart-warming to know
that Beau cared about her feelings. As well as everything else, he'd insisted on arranging driving lessons,
which she'd duly taken—with Wallace aiding and
abetting—so she also had a provisional driver's
licence. She was suddenly, wonderfully, overwhelmed
with identification papers, all of which were now
securely tucked away in her newly bought traveller's
handbag.

Mrs. Featherfield pulled back and dabbed at her
eyes. "Well, we mustn't keep them waiting. I'll carry
your coat. You look so smart in those clothes, it
would be a pity to clutter you up before Master Beau
sees you."

Maggie's heart instantly kicked into overdrive. She
had tried not to think of how alone together she was
going to be with Beau on this trip. He had booked
separate rooms, as promised, and he hadn't once pre-
sumed on the attraction between them. Both of them
did their best to ignore it, yet it was there, stronger
than ever for Maggie since Beau's attitude no longer
carried any discernible trace of hostility. Sooner or
later the temptation to give in to expressing it was
bound to arise.

Would it be right or wrong?

She'd know when it came, she nervously assured herself.

Beau and Sedgewick were in the stairhall. Both of them turned to watch her come down as she and Mrs. Featherfield reached the balcony landing. Benevolent approval was written all over the butler's face. Beau looked relaxed and happy. Nevertheless, Maggie felt there was more than a simmer of pleasure in his eyes as they skimmed her appearance.

She'd donned comfortable clothes, as advised, teaming black trousers and skivvy with a leopard-print velvet vest, a gold-buckled belt and her gold anchor-chain. The outfit wasn't spectacular, just well put together, as Vivian had taught her. It was Beau's gaze on her that made her feel it was sensational and sexy.

Or maybe it was because he looked that way to her, dressed in sage green trousers, a fawn ribbed skivvy, and a dark brown leather jacket, casually hooked over one shoulder. He had such a magnificent physique, it was difficult not to let her gaze linger on his powerfully muscled body.

"I take it all the luggage is already in the car," she said brightly, trying to settle the flutters in her stomach with a concentration on practicalities.

"Wallace has it stowed and is standing by," Beau answered, grinning at the efficiency with which everyone was seeing them off. It was impossible to be unaware of the staff conspiracy to encourage every move towards a harmonious and happy togetherness.

"Perhaps you will send us the occasional postcard, Nanny Stowe," Sedgewick said, his eyebrows raised in pointed appeal.

Wanting to be kept posted on any promising developments, Maggie interpreted. "Of course I will, Sedgewick," she assured him, hoping her smile didn't look as stiff as it felt.

Both he and Mrs. Featherfield escorted them out to the car. Mr. Polly was standing beside Wallace, waiting for them, intent on adding his good wishes to everyone else's.

"Mr. Vivian always reckoned the gardens at Versailles were something special. Should have a look at them when you get to Paris," he advised.

"We will," Beau promised.

"You have a good time now, Nanny Stowe. Mr. Vivian would be real pleased about Master Beau taking you off around the world."

"Thank you, Mr. Polly. I can't imagine I'll see any roses better than yours..." He *had* won first prize at the Royal Easter Show with his Double Delight. "...But I will check out the gardens in Europe."

He nodded and smiled. "Bit of care. That's all it takes," he said as Wallace ushered her into the back seat of the Rolls.

Beau said his last goodbyes and settled onto the seat beside her. Wallace shut the door and with an air of a dignified custodian in control of his charges. He saluted those who'd delivered them to him, took the driver's seat, and set the trip in motion.

"Got the tickets?" Beau asked her, his green eyes twinkling with good humour.

A nanny's job in travelling, he'd declared, was to look after tickets, see that schedules were kept, ensure that nothing was left in planes, trains, restaurants and hotels, hold ready supplies of first-aid items and emergency medications, and generally see that proper meals were taken so appropriate energy levels were maintained.

Maggie suspected that putting her in charge of the tickets was meant to make her feel she always had a passport to freedom. Beau would not hold her with him. The choice was hers.

She patted her handbag. "All correct and double-checked." A blissful sigh of satisfaction accompanied the welling sense of a dream turning into fact. "We're really on our way."

Beau laughed. "You'll feel even more so once the plane takes off. It's always a buzz."

It reminded Maggie that Beau was more than a seasoned traveller. Exploring the world was what he'd chosen to do with his life. She wondered how he thought fatherhood would fit into it, whether he imagined her and their child tagging along with him wherever he went.

On the other hand, when he'd proposed marriage, he'd linked Rosecliff with it, so maybe he envisaged settling there for a while. Or settling *her* there with the child while he came and went. Maggie wasn't sure she liked that idea but it was premature to be considering it anyway. This was a time for gathering a true sense of what life with Beau Prescott might be like.

"I checked the weather report for London, sir. They're having a very cool spring. Nine to fifteen degrees Celsius. You'll have to be snuggling up," Wallace cheerily advised.

"Thank you, Wallace. We do have coats with us," Beau dryly replied.

"Same in Paris and Berlin. Much warmer in Rome.

Twenty-four degrees Celsius there. You'll be able to thaw out once you're in sunny Italy. Won't need your heavy clothes on.''

"I dare say it will be a pleasant change," Maggie commented, hoping Wallace wouldn't go so far as to suggest stripping off entirely.

"Speaking of Italy, I saw a TV program on the Amalfi Coast the other night," he went on. "A couple zooming around in a red Ferrari. Great car. They stopped at a fantastic village that was built like it was hanging on to a cliff. Positano it was called. Looked very romantic.''

"Well, we may make it there," Beau said agreeably.

Wallace continued to be a font of information all the way to the airport. He didn't precisely suggest Beau and Maggie become lovers but the implication was in everything he said. Maggie tried not to feel awkward about it. Beau was very smooth in making light of the more pointed comments. Nevertheless, the pressure to deliver on the promise got to her again.

It was a relief to say goodbye to Wallace but she was hopelessly tense once she was alone with Beau, keeping a rigid distance so there'd be no accidental touching in the airport terminal, fumbling with the tickets at the check-in counter, looking anywhere but directly at him. She found herself tongue-tied, too, nodding when he spoke to her, unable to offer any conversation as they made their way to the first-class lounge to await their flight.

She had a craven urge to run away. People in power make prisons but people you care about also make prisons, she thought. Before coming to Rosecliff, she'd only been responsible for herself. She hadn't let herself become too emotionally involved with anyone or any place. Now she couldn't shrug off those who cared about her and she also had to consider what was best for the baby. Running away wasn't really an option anymore. It wouldn't be fair.

She took a chair by the window in the lounge and stared out at a line of huge jet aeroplanes, waiting for their loads of passengers and cargoes. The only plane she'd ever been in was a four-seat Cessna, commonly used in the Australian outback. How these enormous machines lifted off the ground was a marvel. Soon she would be on one, flying off to the other side of the world. But not alone.

Never alone again, she thought, one hand straying to her stomach. She'd missed a period and the tightness in her breasts was another physical manifestation of her pregnancy. The changes in her body heralded changes in her life she couldn't turn back from. Nor did she want to. Yet she couldn't help feeling apprehensive about the future.

Beau brought her a cup of tea—she'd gone off coffee—and settled into the armchair beside hers. She muttered a "Thank you," still not looking him in the eye.

"You don't have to live up to others' expectations, Maggie," he said quietly. "Especially if it creates a conflict within yourself."

She glanced up, oddly relieved he understood.

He caught her gaze and transmitted an empathy that stroked her troubled heart. "Stay true to whatever you believe is right for you," he advised. "In the end, that's what works best. For everyone. An unhappy person spreads unhappiness."

She recognised the truth in what he said and felt the strength of mind and purpose he'd harnessed to follow his own path in life. In this respect, he was very similar to his grandfather, a natural leader, exuding confidence. It didn't matter that he poured his energy into something different to Vivian. The charismatic power that drew others to him was the same. It made them feel safe within the radius of such strength.

He has a generous heart. Just like his grandfather. You'll be safe with him, dear.

The insight suddenly burst upon her. "It's you they need, not me. Do you realise that, Beau?"

"You mean Feathers and Sedgewick and…"

"Yes. Vivian was the focus of their lives. They're clinging on to him through me because…" She hesitated, reluctant to starkly state what they wanted of her.

"They see you as a way to hold on to their lives at Rosecliff," he said, openly revealing his perception and encouraging her to speak hers.

She leaned forward, earnestly pressing the truth she had just comprehended. "It's not the place so much. It's you. You're Vivian's natural heir, and I'm not referring to simply inheriting his property. They want you to give their lives purpose, providing a hub for them to work around as your grandfather did, and they're afraid you won't, afraid you'll let them go and they won't know what to do then."

"You don't have to worry about that, Maggie.

They're my family. One way or another, I'll answer their needs. You can count on it.''

In so saying, he lifted all responsibility from her shoulders and the burden on her heart. She sat back and smiled, happy he understood.

They *were* safe with him.

Beau had made her feel very unsafe but she realised now he had felt unsafe with her, too. It had been right to tell him about herself, good to clear the air between them. She relaxed, enjoying a sense of freedom in exploring more with him.

"Any other worries?' he asked, obviously wanting to erase her fears.

"No. Except..." She nodded to the view outside the window. "...I hope our plane doesn't crash."

He grinned. "We're flying with an airline that has an excellent safety record."

"Those jumbo jets are so huge."

"I'll hold your hand."

She laughed as warmth flooded through her. Maybe she and their child would be safe in his keeping. A strong man with a generous heart would surely make a good father. Would he be her mate for life?

An hour later Maggie was strapped into a spacious and comfortable window seat, being treated to the privileges of a first-class passenger on a flight to London. The plane was zooming down the runway, picking up enormous speed. Just as she was tensing for the lift-off, Beau reached over and took her hand.

She felt the warmth and comfort of the reassuring gesture as she watched the ground fall away beneath them and experienced the exhilaration of climbing up to the sky. Once she was confident they were not about to drop out of it, she turned her head from the window and smiled at the man who was looking after her, her whole body humming with a wonderful sense of sharing.

"My grandfather called this the great adventure," he said, returning her smile.

"Thank you for taking me on it, Beau."

In more ways than one, she thought, looking down at their linked hands, liking the togetherness.

It was a journey towards trust.

The greatest adventure of all.

And the most dangerous.

CHAPTER FIFTEEN

BEAU very quickly understood his grandfather's enchantment with Maggie Stowe. She was so eager for knowledge, she soaked up everything she could, loving the experience of a wider world, the wonder of it sparkling in her eyes. Fatigue, hunger, discomfort...none of it meant anything to her if there was something more to take in and savour. London was a historical feast and even its present living culture was endlessly fascinating to her.

She wasn't a tourist as Beau knew tourists, notching up places they'd been. She wasn't interested in buying souvenirs, nor even looking at them. That took up time better spent in active pursuit of a bigger treasure house of memories to be kept in her mind and heart and soul. So she said.

Beau suspected she automatically dismissed souvenirs as excess baggage. In a life led *travelling lightly,* books and ornaments would simply weigh her down. She didn't have a family home where she could store them. What most people took for granted had not been available to Maggie Stowe.

To have carried through such an isolated and alienated existence and still have an open-hearted zest for exploring more and more of life, showed a truly amazing resilience. Gutsy and grand, Beau thought, and found himself admiring her more than he usually admired anyone.

Even with places he had already seen, she revitalised his interest and extended it. He remembered on his previous visit to the Tower of London with his grandfather, he'd been captivated by its fortress aspect, the rooms where famous people had been imprisoned, the instruments of torture, suits of armour. Maggie was more enthralled with the Queens of England who'd been buried in the chapel, and shocked by the wealth of the British Empire, embedded in the Crown Jewels.

It was fun to be with her. She brought a kind of magical joy to each day with her vibrant enthusiasm, a dancing smile and evocative comments inviting him to share everything that touched her. He loved her uninhibited reactions, enjoyed her perceptions, found intense pleasure in her company, and thought how much he'd like spending the rest of his life with her.

He took her to Harrods since a visit to London wouldn't be complete without a look at the famous store. It was a natural expectation that Maggie would be tempted into buying something from the rich array of goods on display, if only one of the exotic pastries from the food hall. She did end up making a purchase, but not for herself, for Sedgewick.

"Look, Beau! A silver stopper for bottles of champagne. It's to keep the bubbles in after the bottle's been opened." Her eyes sparkled with glee. "Sedgewick will love it!"

"Why?" he asked, bemused by her pleasure in it.

"Oh, he looks so pained when nobody wants any more champagne and there's still some left in the bottle. With this stopper he can keep it for later and enjoy it himself. He never drinks while he's on duty and he hates waste. I must buy it for him.''

She was being served when she was struck by second thoughts, turning to Beau in agitated uncertainty. "Maybe I shouldn't. You don't drink champagne as Vivian did. If you don't intend to throw any more parties or do functions at Rosecliff..."

"Buy it," he said decisively. When still she doubted, he added, "I won't be dropping my grandfather's charity balls. If I'm not there to host them, I'll put Sedgewick in charge."

And on such an off-the-cuff incident, the future of Rosecliff suddenly turned. Or maybe the decision had been building up in him from the day he'd first returned home to a heritage he couldn't quite disown. Rosecliff represented home to him and having a home with a sense of continuity to it had a value now it didn't have before getting to know Maggie Stowe. Every child deserved a proper family home and Beau was determined on giving their child the best he could offer.

Having said what he'd said, it felt right. He'd make it happen. And Maggie was an integral part of it. Somehow he'd make her realise that before this trip was over.

They caught the Eurostar train from Waterloo to Paris, travelling under the English Channel and speeding across the countryside of France faster than any cars they saw on the roads. They both gave the trip top marks for inclusion on a tour.

To Beau, in his teens, Paris had been a city of stupendous grandeur, dominated by the architectural splendour of its public buildings and monuments, the marvellous precision of their mathematical alignment, the spirit of Napoleon and the fantastic Eiffel Tower. He hadn't seen it as a romantic city for lovers. He did now.

Spring in Paris. There was a nip in the air as Wallace had forewarned but the sun shone on them as he and Maggie followed the walking tours he'd planned; enjoying the pretty tree-lined streets that led up to the Sacre-Coeur, stopping to watch the clever acts of mime artists; strolling from the Louvre, through the Tuileries and all the way down the Champs-Élysées, pausing to cast a critical eye over an exhibition of sculptures, admiring the massed displays of flowers in the gardens, having fun simply people-watching.

On the very first day, he'd caught her hand when she'd stumbled over uneven cobblestones. He hadn't relinquished it and she hadn't withdrawn it. The tacit acceptance emboldened him to take her hand every day. Beau could hardly believe how good it felt...this least intimate of physical links. In his mind he tied it to liking, approval, acceptance and respect, and his heart swelled with the sense of achievement this gave him. He was breaking down the barriers between them, winning her trust.

They spent a day at Versailles, marvelling at the incredible artistry involved in supplying the best of everything to the Sun-King of France; the riches of the palace, the extravagance of Le Trianon, the breathtaking design of the forest and fountains and gardens. Maggie bought a book of photographs of the latter to give to Mr. Polly.

"Just to satisfy his curiosity," she remarked. "He's

such a master gardener himself, he'll appreciate the attention to detail in all of this."

Another day, they wandered around an antique fair, set up along the banks of the Seine near the Bastille. On one of the stalls Maggie saw a collection of elaborately designed brass buttons. "For Wallace," she cried excitedly. "He'd just love these on his chauffeur's uniform. Help me choose, Beau. I'll buy them and sew them on his jacket for him."

"You're right," he agreed, surprised by her perception. "Short of a red Ferrari, you couldn't buy him anything better. Wallace will be puffing his chest out everywhere."

They both grinned over the little vanity, enjoying their shared knowledge of the chauffeur's pride in his uniform. Once again Beau was touched by Maggie's thoughtfulness in the gift.

He was further struck by her caring perception when she pulled him into a lingerie boutique in the Place des Voges. He initially thought she was finally going to buy something for herself, but it was Mrs. Featherfield she had in mind.

"A nightgown from Paris with real French lace. She'll adore it, Beau."

The saleswoman obligingly laid out several on the counter. Beau eyed the sexy gown Maggie was fingering, trying to see it objectively instead of envisaging her in it. So far he'd managed to keep his desire for her under control, but willpower couldn't quell the needs she stirred and the display of highly erotic lingerie was dangerously arousing.

"You don't think that's a bit...well, Feathers isn't exactly young and she is rather buxom," he commented critically, thinking the sooner they got out of this shop, the better.

Maggie laughed, her eyes teasing his ignorance. "A woman is never too old or plump to enjoy feeling feminine and deliciously sensual," she declared knowingly. "Mrs. Featherfield loves the nightie I..."

She stopped, biting her lips as heat flared into her cheeks. Beau knew instantly what she was remembering. The image of her in the navy silk and lace gown burst into his mind, tempting him beyond endurance. He sensed her own sharp awareness of it, the flash flood of desire sweeping through her, the struggle to contain it. A wild exultation possessed him. It was the same for her...the want...the need...*the same for her!*

Beau didn't pause to question the compulsion that seized him. He swept the array of nighties on the counter over his arm. "Trying them on," he threw at the saleswoman, nodding to the change cubicles at the back of the shop. He scooped Maggie along with him and she came unresistingly, hustled into movement, catching her breath, looking hotly confused but not protesting.

His heart was hammering as he yanked the curtain of the cubicle closed behind them and tossed the nightgowns on a padded stool. His whole body was tingling with feverish anticipation as he turned to gather Maggie to him. She dropped the bags she'd been holding, her emptied hands lifting, but not to push him away. No. They slid inside his jacket, wanting to touch, wanting to feel him, and the intense yearning in her eyes set him on fire.

He wrapped her in his arms and kissed her with all

the pent-up hunger of weeks pouring into a passionate need for her wholehearted response. She left him in no doubt of it, her mouth as urgent as his in tasting and accelerating the intensity of sensation generated by their mutual desire for each other. He covered her face with kisses, breathed in the seductive scent of her hair, moved her back against the wall for support as they both trembled with the force of their release from the restriction they'd imposed on themselves.

With his hands free to revel in the soft curves of her femininity, his mouth sought hers again, loving it, caressing it, savouring its hot sensuality. It was like drinking champagne on an empty stomach. His head swam with the exhilarating intoxication of it and he couldn't put a stopper on the bottle. Her arms were around his neck, her body arched excitingly against his, her fingers curling into his hair, holding him to her, wanting him.

His erection was painfully hard, fighting the constriction of his jeans, throbbing for release, desperately seeking its home within the soft cradle of her hips. And Maggie was burrowing closer to him, the thrust of her breasts pressing deliciously against his chest, her stomach curling around his hard shaft, relishing it, inviting him, encouraging him, the quiver of her thighs revealing the same feverish desire that gripped him.

His hands scrabbled at the cloth of her long skirt until they found the hem and pulled it up. Then came the fierce delight of finding she was wearing garterless stockings, not tights, and the silky scrap of her panties gave easy access to the intimacy he craved. She was already wet with need for him, and she shuddered and gasped as he stroked her.

A purring sound came from her throat, music to Beau's ears, but not to hers. Her eyes opened wide, the sudden realisation of where they were and what was being done rocketing through the sensual haze of satisfaction.

''Beau, we can't...'' The shocked whisper fell from lips swollen with his kisses and tremulous with a denial she didn't really want to make. Her body was straining to give, to feel all he would give her.

''Maggie, I'm dying for you...'' He pinned her skirt up with his thighs and tore his zip open.

Then as he guided his own hot flesh along the soft path of her other lips, already so sexually aroused they welcomed him in convulsive ecstasy, she sighed with exquisite pleasure, ''Yes...yes...'' and her eyes swam with sweet relief and a wild, reckless acceptance of any time, place or circumstance.

She lifted a leg, opening herself further, sensuously stroking his leg with it. Only a shallow penetration was possible and the teasing of it was driving him crazy with excitement. He shoved his jeans down his thighs, filled his hands with the soft roundness of her buttocks and hoisted her up, the explosive tension inside him demanding the thrust that took him deep inside her, fast and strong and intensely fulfilling.

She wound her legs around his hips, sinking him even further. And there was a moment to die for, a moment of stillness, of exquisite appreciation of how it was to be together like this, so deeply co-joined, owning an inner world that was uniquely theirs, that drummed only to their beat.

Her hands clutched his shoulders, fingers digging into his flesh as though they, too, would claw inside, holding and possessing what they shared by any primitive means. Her head was thrown back, exposing her long throat, and there at the base of it her pulse visibly throbbed. He kissed it, drew on it, loving the sense of her heart thrumming with his.

He felt her muscles start to spasm around him and he abandoned the kiss to ride the gathering storm of sensation, driving ahead of it, pushing it, rushing along with it, plunging from crest to crest, as the waves of her climax rolled through him and the sheer wild glory of it caught up with him and spilled him into the sweet peace of heaven.

She slumped over him, hugging his head, and he buried his face in the heaving softness of her breasts. He wrapped her fiercely in his arms to prevent her slipping away from him, holding on to their intimacy as long as he could. Her fingers stroked his neck as though gentling him and he felt a rush of tenderness for the woman she was, the mother she would be.

He listened to her heartbeat, feeling an emotional intensity he'd never felt before. This woman belonged to him. He would never let her go. Never. He would fight whatever he had to fight to keep her.

Only when she stirred did he become aware of external sounds; footsteps, a burst of conversation in French, the click of hangers on racks. "Beau..." she whispered, her breath warm on his skin, fingers stroking his hair, alerting him to the shift that had to be made.

She leaned back against the wall. He lifted his head. Her face was flushed, her eyes brilliantly luminous, her mouth slightly parted as though her lips were too sensitised to close. She met his gaze unflinchingly, locking on to it, determined on open honesty yet unable to hide a shimmer of intense vulnerability.

"Other customers have come in. This isn't exactly a safe place," she murmured shakily.

"Doesn't matter. They're strangers we'll never meet again," he answered. "This...us...is far more important, Maggie."

Her smile was wry. "I can't believe I let this happen again. It's crazy."

"But you wanted it," Beau pressed, alarmed at the thought of her backing off from him.

"Yes," she said helplessly.

His fear dissolved into a relieved and happy grin. "Maybe it seemed crazy the first time, when we didn't really know each other, but this time it makes perfect sense."

She giggled. "In a change cubicle?"

"Marks a change, doesn't it?"

She shook her head in bemusement. "I didn't imagine change would come quite like this."

She accepted it though, Beau thought exultantly. "Spontaneous combustion," he explained. "I promise I'll romance you tonight. How about a dinner cruise on the Seine? The lights of Paris, seductive food, French champagne..."

Her eyes softened. She stroked his cheek. "You don't have to, Beau. It's not really about romance, is it?"

"No. It's about what we give to each other. Very basic. But there's no reason we can't put a shine on it, Maggie, and I want to give you all the highlights the world has to offer.'' He meant it, too. There was nothing glib about what he felt for her.

She expelled a deep sigh. To his ears it was the sound of contentment in their understanding. Her eyes flirted with the confidence he'd imparted. ''Well, I think it's time you put my feet back on the ground so we can resume our journey.''

He kissed her to make up for the more intimate disconnection and there was no awkwardness at all about fixing themselves up before rejoining the public world. Acceptance, approval, liking, respect, Beau happily recited to himself as he waited for Maggie to complete the purchase of a sinful piece of sensuality for Mrs. Featherfield.

There was one thing wrong with the list, he decided. *Liking* wasn't strong enough.

He *loved* Maggie Stowe.

He felt he couldn't bear her out of his sight, let alone out of his life. It wasn't simply the part of him she carried inside her—their child—that made it essential to convince her that marriage to him could never conceivably be a prison. It was the person she was…his mate in every sense he could think of. He wanted—*needed* from her—the commitment of marriage.

CHAPTER SIXTEEN

IT WAS strange for Maggie to be so *close* to another person. It felt right. Everything with Beau now *felt* right. But it was strange, having someone close who seemed to understand whatever was going on in her mind, who could virtually anticipate her impulses, who was constantly there for her.

She wasn't used to it. She'd never had a relationship like this. Even the mental affinity and affection she'd shared with Vivian did not approach the depth of this closeness with Beau. She missed Vivian, but she had never doubted she could go on without him. With Beau it was different. He pervaded almost every breath she breathed, giving it a buoyant happiness she had never known. Take him away...she shied from thinking about that, afraid of how bereft she might feel.

Enjoy the moment, she kept telling herself. Worrying about tomorrow was a waste of the present. Maybe she was living in a fool's paradise, but it was paradise.

The days were filled with amazing sights; the towering black cathedral at Cologne, the fairytale castles along the Rhine River, the majestic mountains of Austria. Once they reached Italy, it became impossible to categorise the sheer romance of the places they explored...Lake Como, Verona, Venice with its intriguing history and location.

The nights were so intimate, Maggie forgot what it

171

was like to be alone. Which was scary, since she had spent so many years on her own. Even when she had shared rooms, slept in dormitories of bunks, or camped out with a group, the sense of being an independent individual had never left her. Yet the longer she was with Beau, the more blurred became the line of separation between them.

From Paris onwards, he had rebooked their accommodation. Separate rooms were pointless. Neither of them wanted to be parted. There were moments when just looking at him—this man who excited all her senses—evoked the most extraordinary feelings of intense possessiveness.

He was a lover of great tenderness, as well as passion. He could draw her into sex, into *loving,* with a slow gentleness that eased her into new territories, new discoveries about herself, then take her with him to heights so wild and wonderful, her body would lurch with delight at the memory of it for days afterwards. He was inventive, thoughtful, responsive, challenging, and she didn't have the slightest regret about giving in to the sexual attraction she'd wanted to explore with him. However, she did sometimes wonder if its potency coloured everything else they shared.

How long did passion last?

She had no answer to that question. No one to ask. No one to tell her. Impossible to bring it up with Beau. She couldn't forget he had a vested interest in tying her to him, so how could she trust anything he said about the future? She could only trust what she knew they felt together now.

He rented a villa in Tuscany, intending it as a base for forays into Florence and other outings around the beautiful countryside. The villa was situated on a hill, giving a lovely view of olive groves and green fields dotted with wild red poppies. Maggie was instantly captivated by the soft quality of the light in Tuscany. It seemed to deepen colours and spread a magical sense of peace and well-being.

Having been situated in cities for most of their travelling, their move to the quiet and slower pace of this relaxing location had a strong appeal. It was also timely for Maggie. Apart from the tightness in her breasts, she had barely been aware of her pregnancy. Morning sickness hit with debilitating results.

At first she struggled to carry on as Beau's tour companion, but three days of trying to ignore how unwell she felt, proved the impossibility of this endeavour. Each morning she had to ask Beau to stop their rental car so she could be sick on the side of the road. They missed out on getting into the Uffizi Palace in Florence because standing in the long queue for over an hour had resulted in her fainting. An unfightable fatigue swept over her in the afternoons, sapping her enthusiasm for sightseeing, and she dropped off to sleep during the return trips to the villa.

Beau's kindness and patience and consideration for her were exemplary but she felt miserably guilty for holding him up, wasting his time and giving him the general unpleasantness of worrying about her. On the fourth day, she decided to beg off going anywhere, too conscious of being a drag on him to enjoy being a tourist.

When she'd rolled out of bed, the room had spun, forcing her to lie down again and keep very still until everything righted itself. Beau had gone to make her a cup of tea, hoping it would help to settle the queaziness she felt. When he came back, he was frowning in concern.

"Would you like to see a doctor, Maggie?" he asked, setting the tea on the bedside table. "Maybe you need iron tablets or..."

"No, I'll be fine soon," she quickly assured him, hating the thought of causing any fuss. "I'm sure this is just a phase, Beau. I'm sorry it's inconveniencing you."

"Inconveniencing..." It was plain he didn't like the word, stiffening up and looking sharply at her.

Maggie sighed her impatience with any pretence. She didn't feel like arguing the point so she simply said, "I want to stay here today, Beau. There's no need to worry about me. I'll just lie around and relax and..."

"Are you suggesting I leave you here and go off to Sienna as planned?" he broke in tersely.

"Why not? I'm perfectly capable of looking after myself," she answered reasonably.

"Even if you are, it's a hell of a judgment on me, Maggie, sending me off as though I wouldn't care about you."

He was offended, she realised, deeply offended by her assumption he would leave her to her own resources in these circumstances. As she stared at him, taking in his viewpoint, his face twisted with frustration.

"Damn it, Maggie! I said I'd look after you. It's you who's insisted on carrying on these past few days. Do you think I've enjoyed watching you push yourself?"

She frowned, confused by this further critical note

on her handling of the situation. Didn't he realise she'd been considering his needs?

He gestured hopelessly and turned away, walking to the end of the bed. His shoulders heaved and he swung around, his face anguished by some inner torment. "I kept telling myself to respect your right to make your own decisions, but I have the same right, Maggie, so don't take it upon yourself to make decisions for me. Your welfare and that of our child is as much my responsibility as it is yours. It's wrong for you to take that away from me, too."

"Beau, this is a business trip for you," she reminded him.

"Is that your excuse for holding yourself in and shutting me out?" he threw at her.

Maggie stared at him in bewilderment.

He expelled a sigh of deep exasperation and shook his head. "You still don't trust me, do you?" he said dully, the anger gone as abruptly as it had burst forth.

"I'm not sure I know what you mean," she said tentatively.

His bleak look smote her heart. "Never mind. I'm sorry for losing my temper when you're not well." He grimaced. "I never seem to get my timing right with you."

"That's not true." It was more an offer of appeasement than a comment.

"Isn't it?" He shrugged and walked to the door. He paused there a moment, then looked back, his eyes raking hers with pain. "If you want anything, call out. I'll be in hearing range. As unbelievable as you might find it, Maggie, business doesn't come first with me. You do. You and our child. You always will."

He left her with that quiet statement of fact and

Maggie couldn't block a rush of tears. A huge lump of emotion constricted her throat. It was impossible to call him back right then, and perhaps it was better not to. She needed time to think, to sort herself out in the light of how Beau perceived her.

For a while, her mind couldn't move past his assertion that she came first with him. She and their child. It was such a huge thing to comprehend. She hadn't expected him—anyone—to put her needs ahead of his...to care so much...for her to be so important to him.

She'd never been that important to anybody.

She'd stifled the urge to cling to him this morning, to ask him to stay with her, dismissing it as silly weakness and unfair to him. Now the accusation of holding herself in and shutting him out hit home. She had been doing that, automatically shying away from expecting anything of him, not *trusting*.

Yet what was there not to trust in Beau? What more did he have to prove to her? Hadn't he done everything he said he would? And given her much more!

So they'd had an unfortunate start. He'd explained what he'd felt and why he'd acted as he had. He'd more than compensated for his errors in judgment where she was concerned. It was wrong not to trust him.

He'd left the bedroom door open. She was free to call on him anytime. He'd invited her to. There was no reason to feel inhibited about it. Whether he responded or not was his decision, his choice. It finally dawned on her that without open communication, trust couldn't grow and she was denying any chance of that with second-guessing him, as well as burying her head in the sand rather than look at the future.

Maggie sipped the tea Beau had brought her as new resolutions formed in her mind. He'd put some cookies on the saucer. She ate one slowly, testing her stomach's reaction. Feeling no ill effects, she finished the lot, then tentatively got out of bed again.

The world remained normal.

She dressed quickly and went in search of Beau. He was sitting at the table under the vine-covered pergola which spread along the front of the villa. A notebook and Biro were at hand but he wasn't writing anything, just staring out at the view, apparently in deep thought.

When she stepped out on the flagstoned terrace, his head jerked around as though he had been listening for any noise, reacting instantly to it. The tension in his body leapt out at her. She hesitated, suddenly uncertain of her welcome. Then he visibly relaxed, his mouth curling into an ironic smile as his gaze swept over her appearance.

"Well, I guess you've shown you didn't need my help."

"Yes, I did," she quickly corrected. "The tea and cookies helped a lot. I feel much better now."

"Glad to hear it." He gestured to a chair. "It's very pleasant sitting out here. Would you care to join me?"

She nodded. "Don't get up. I'm fine now. Really."

He subsided in his seat and watched her sit down. Maggie's nerves jangled. Had she done the wrong thing again, rejecting the courtesy of seeing her seated? Heat rushed into her cheeks and just as quickly receded, reflecting the emotional mess she was in.

"I'm sorry I offended you earlier," she gabbled, her eyes pleading his forgiveness. "I didn't mean to make you feel unwanted. I'm just not used to...to depending on other people.''

He shrugged. ''No need to apologise. It's not your fault. I do appreciate it's difficult for you, Maggie. With your background.''

He turned his gaze away to the view spread out below them. Maggie wanted to dismiss his reference to her past, yet it was relevant. Somehow his sympathy and understanding shamed her. She shouldn't be letting the far past taint her judgment. There were no points of comparison to it in her relationship with Beau. None at all.

''My grandfather used to call me the wild child,'' he said whimsically. ''Not undeserved. But I think the name more aptly fits you.''

''Me?' Maggie frowned, not seeing the parallel.

He sliced her a darkly knowing look. ''Not even the compound could tame you, Maggie. And you've been roaming free ever since you got out of there.''

Only because I never felt I really belonged anywhere, she thought.

He shifted his attention back to the view. ''I was looking down at that field of poppies earlier, before you came out. All those flowers growing wild and free, so vibrant with their red petals. The thought came to me that they probably wouldn't thrive nearly so well, transplanted to a formal garden. Better to let them grow their own way. Let them shine how they will.''

She sensed melancholy and despair and inwardly railed against the darkness falling between them. He was withdrawing from her. She could feel it. He swung his gaze to her again and she saw it, the deep personal pain behind the restraint he was grimly holding.

"I've done everything wrong with you, Maggie. I thought I could right it. Sheer blind arrogance on my part." He managed a travesty of a smile. "The pushing stops here. If you want us to lead separate lives...well, it's up to you to decide on what arrangement suits you best."

She understood then. It was she who'd been blind. Beau loved her. And she had wounded his generous heart to the point of giving up on ever winning her love. She also knew words would be meaningless, as meaningless as they'd been to her without the right actions to back them up.

She rose from her chair, her heart gripped by a panicky urgency. She had to prove to him that all his gifts of love to her had not been in vain. She had learnt. The past was not going to blight her life with him. It wasn't going to touch them anymore.

Without a word she turned and walked away, heading straight down the hill to the field of red poppies. A feverish energy pumped through her veins. A sense of destiny pounded through her brain. Beau Prescott was her mate. She was going to spend the rest of her life with him. She was not going to be afraid of anything.

Once amongst the wildflowers, she stooped to pick a bouquet of them, gathering them up as fast as she could. When she had an armful, she took a deep breath to steady herself, then started the return journey to the villa.

It startled her to see Beau had followed her and was standing only a few metres away, watching her intently, obviously worried over her physical or men-

tal state. She smiled to ease his concern and headed
straight for him. There was puzzlement in his eyes as
she offered him the bouquet of poppies.

"I give them into your keeping, Beau," she softly
explained, her eyes begging him to understand. "With
them comes my absolute trust. And my love. And my
life."

"Maggie…" Hope conflicted with doubt.

"Please?"

"Dear God!" He took the flowers, though his eyes
said they were no substitute for her. "I thought…"

"I think we do much better together when we stop
thinking, Beau."

He laughed and tossed the poppies aside to wrap
her in his arms. "I love you, Maggie Stowe. You are
where I want to be for the rest of my life."

Her heart caught, then soared. She slid her arms
around his neck, pressing closer as she kissed him,
the great surge of feeling between them pouring into
the swift, fierce passion they had known from the very
beginning. For a long, long time, they lay amongst
the wild poppies in the field, bathed in the soft mys-
tical light of Tuscany, loving each other in the full
knowledge of their love.

Not once did Maggie think of Vivian's wishes. Nor
did she think of Rosecliff or those wanting this happy
outcome, nor of the child conceived before either she
or Beau had considered such a possibility. She
thought only of being with this man, where she would
always belong. This was *their* chance, and she didn't
want to waste a moment of it.

CHAPTER SEVENTEEN

ST. ANDREW'S Cathedral was packed for what was being called The Wedding of the Year—Beau Prescott, heir to the Prescott millions and owner of Rosecliff, marrying his grandfather's beautiful protégé, Margaret Stowe, with the bishop performing the ceremony and the boys' choir giving voice to songs of joy.

It was what Mr. Vivian would have wanted, Sedgewick had declared, informing Beau and Maggie in no uncertain terms, and volubly backed up by Mrs. Featherfield, Wallace and Mr. Polly, that this wedding had to be the grandest party of them all.

Beau smiled to himself as he waited at the head of the aisle for his bride to appear. He hadn't argued with them. He wanted to give Maggie the best of everything, especially on their wedding day. And no way would he spoil the pleasure of the faithful four in contributing to the event.

Sedgewick was undoubtedly in his element, supervising all the arrangements in the ballroom at Rosecliff, getting ready to distribute oceans of the best French champagne. Feathers would have revelled in helping Maggie to dress. Wallace would be as proud as punch, chauffeuring the bride in the most brilliantly polished Rolls in the city. Mr. Polly's roses were on prime display and would undoubtedly feature in Maggie's bouquet.

They were all delighted with his and Maggie's

plans for the future, too, keeping Rosecliff as their home and a centre for supporting his grandfather's charities, while taking time away each year to explore and organise a new package tour for their travel agency. Beau couldn't help grinning as he remembered planning this with Maggie.

"We will have a child to consider," she'd reminded him.

"Any child with our genes is bound to be a wild child," he'd declared. "It will just be one big adventure after another."

"You mean we take our family with us?"

"Why not? We'll open all the windows on the world."

To which she'd laughingly agreed.

And he'd teasingly added, "Of course we'll need a nanny to come with us to give us time to ourselves. Or for the occasional short trip, we can leave nanny and child at home for Feathers and Sedgewick and Wallace and Mr. Polly to spoil outrageously."

With which *they* had heartily agreed.

The fulsome tones of the pipe organ faded into silence. Beau's heart kicked. This was it. He turned as the first chords of Mendelssohn's "Wedding March" rang through the cathedral. And there she was, hugging Sir Roland's arm, starting down the long aisle towards him.

At first he thought she looked like a Medieval princess. Her high-waisted ivory silk gown was embroidered in gold and rich in elegance, shimmering with each step she took. Then he focused on her radiant face, framed by her glorious hair and haloed by her bridal veil and he thought...an angel. The Angel of Life.

The dress artfully covered her four months' pregnancy but the thought of the child she carried in her womb—their child—filled Beau with a special sense of awe as he watched her come to him. The words his grandfather had once spoken to Lionel Armstrong slid into his mind...creation...salvation...and they suddenly had meaning, beautiful magical meaning.

The family line would go on through him and Maggie. Had his grandfather foreseen that? Was his spirit somewhere close, smiling over them, giving them his blessing?

Then Maggie was beside him, giving him her hand in trust and in love, and Beau held it safe as they pledged themselves to each other, husband and wife. The cathedral filled with song, voices soaring in joyful celebration. It was a pale echo of what they felt in their hearts, what was reflected in their eyes. All the years of their lives had been leading to this moment...the mating that was meant to be...and this was their wedding.

The reception in the ballroom at Rosecliff was every bit as splendid as Sedgewick ordained it should be. It was the most glittering evening anyone could ever remember. Jeffrey cracked the whip over the caterers who served superb food. Champagne flowed. Mrs. Featherfield kept the maids on their toes. The floral arrangements were fantastic. Sir Roland led off the speeches, all of which were warm and witty and wonderful.

When it was time for the Bridal Waltz, because of certain information imparted to Beau by Wallace, the band didn't play a waltz at all. The Bridal Dance was announced and to the opening strains of one of Abba's hit songs, "Dancing Queen," Beau proudly led

Maggie out to the centre of the floor, parading her to the guests who spontaneously and loudly applauded. She was laughing in delight when he turned her into in his arms, the song in full swing as he took her dancing.

"Who told you it was an old favourite of mine?" she asked.

"Wallace. And what more appropriate?" He grinned at her. "I'm dancing with the queen of my heart."

"And I with my king."

The look in her eyes was almost Beau's undoing, especially when the band moved into playing "I do, I do, I do, I do, I do," but he manfully restrained himself from racing his newly wedded wife off to a private place. It was probably fortunate that Sir Roland claimed Maggie for his dance, thus removing temptation.

Lionel Armstrong took the opportunity to draw Beau aside and pass him an envelope. "It's from your grandfather. I was instructed to give it to you in the event of your marriage to Margaret Stowe."

Beau was astounded. "How could he possibly know it would happen?"

"He didn't. I was given another envelope to be handed to you when the stipulated year in the will was up if you hadn't married Margaret Stowe."

Beau shook his head in total bemusement. "So what happens to the second envelope now?"

"It has already been destroyed as per Vivian's instructions. He said the marriage would make it irrelevant. I was further instructed to tell you that this…" he tapped the envelope in Beau's hands "…should be read by both of you on your wedding night."

It gave Beau important cause to whiz Maggie off

to a private place. She was as deeply intrigued as he by this extraordinary action by his grandfather and they sought brief refuge in the library. The envelope contained a letter and a set of keys which puzzled them both, making them all the more eager to read what Vivian Prescott had written.

My dear Beau,
I am delighted you've had the good sense to marry Maggie. She is my wedding present to you since I found her, having despaired of you ever staying still long enough to recognise a soulmate.

Beau chuckled. "The old devil. I bet he was planning this from day one of meeting you."

"You don't mind?" Maggie queried.

"Why should I mind? He got it right."

Her smile glowed with love. "Yes, he did."

They read on...

The keys are to open a safe-deposit box—details next page. In it is my wedding gift to Maggie. She has a need to feel free, Beau, which is a need you must understand if you are to sustain a happy marriage. To ensure this in a financial sense, I have put a million dollars in the box for her to use as she wills.

The missing million!

"Oh!" Maggie slapped her hands to flaming cheeks. "How could he? All that money!"

Beau grinned at her. The mystery was solved at last. "He could because he loved you, Maggie. And that money's going to be yours to do whatever you like with it."

''Well, thank heaven we're married so I won't feel wrong about him giving it to me.''

''You would have had to take it anyway.''

''What?''

''Look for yourself.''

If you had been foolish enough to let Maggie slip away from you, my instruction would have been to give this amount to her so she would never again feel the insecurity she was burdened with through no fault of her own. I trust you would have done that, Beau, without contesting my wish on this matter.

Beau instantly saw his grandfather's wisdom in taking this bequest out of the will. With a year's grace, he wouldn't have begrudged Maggie the million, but faced with it straight away, he probably would have raised even worse hell than he had.

''He was so kind to me,'' was her heartfelt murmur.

''Maggie, you did a lot for him, too,'' Beau assured her, feeling fine about everything until he read the next paragraph.

I have one request to make. When my great-grandson is born, I would like you to follow the tradition of the Prescott family in assigning a name which will develop strength of mind and character and lend a unique individuality to live up to. My personal fancy is Marian.

''Over my dead body!'' Beau growled.

''Marian!'' Maggie exclaimed. ''I thought that was a girl's name.''

''Yes! Like Vivian and Beverly and... Goddamn it!

I am not going to saddle a son of mine with a name like that! Beau was bad enough.''

"I like Beau. It suits you. I liked Vivian, too. It suited him. Maybe…''

"Don't say it! I will not consider Marian.''

"Well, maybe we'll only have daughters.''

"Let's hope.'' He lovingly patted her stomach. "You'd better be a girl in there.''

The letter finished off with his grandfather saying he was now off on the greatest adventure of all and he wished them both the very best of this world.

It left them smiling.

"I guess you could say he came to our wedding,'' Beau said with a warm glow of contentment.

"I think he's been here all day.''

"Yes. But the night is definitely ours, Maggie.''

He drew her into his arms and their kiss excluded everyone else, a long, satisfying private celebration of a togetherness that was uniquely theirs.

Five months later a boy was born.

He was christened Marian John Richard Prescott.

Beau insisted it was up to the boy himself to choose what name he wanted to live with and that his great-grandfather couldn't have his way about everything. In the meantime, Maggie could call him Marian. If she really, really wanted to. He wouldn't deny her that right as long as she understood it was an act of love on his part.

Maggie smiled very lovingly at both him and their son and said she thought family tradition was nice.

Beau remembered she had come from nowhere, saw her need, understood it, and surrendered with a sigh of resignation to the inevitable.

Marian Prescott developed a lot of character.

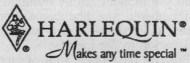

HARLEQUIN ULTIMATE GUIDES™

A series of how-to books for today's woman.

Act now to order some of these extremely
helpful guides just for you!

*Whatever the situation, Harlequin Ultimate Guides™
has all the answers!*

#80507	HOW TO TALK TO A	$4.99 U.S.	☐
	NAKED MAN	$5.50 CAN.	☐
#80508	I CAN FIX THAT	$5.99 U.S.	☐
		$6.99 CAN.	☐
#80510	WHAT YOUR TRAVEL AGENT	$5.99 U.S.	☐
	KNOWS THAT YOU DON'T	$6.99 CAN.	☐
#80511	RISING TO THE OCCASION		
	More Than Manners: Real Life	$5.99 U.S.	☐
	Etiquette for Today's Woman	$6.99 CAN.	☐
#80513	WHAT GREAT CHEFS	$5.99 U.S.	☐
	KNOW THAT YOU DON'T	$6.99 CAN.	☐
#80514	WHAT SAVVY INVESTORS	$5.99 U.S.	☐
	KNOW THAT YOU DON'T	$6.99 CAN.	☐
#80509	GET WHAT YOU WANT OUT OF	$5.99 U.S.	☐
	LIFE—AND KEEP IT!	$6.99 CAN.	☐

(quantities may be limited on some titles)

TOTAL AMOUNT	$	
POSTAGE & HANDLING	$	
($1.00 for one book, 50¢ for each additional)		
APPLICABLE TAXES*	$	_____
TOTAL PAYABLE	$	_____
(check or money order—please do not send cash)		

To order, complete this form and send it, along with a check or money
order for the total above, payable to Harlequin Ultimate Guides, to:
In the U.S.: 3010 Walden Avenue, P.O. Box 9047, Buffalo, NY
14269-9047; **In Canada:** P.O. Box 613, Fort Erie, Ontario, L2A 5X3.

Name: _____

Address: _____ City: _____

State/Prov.: _____ Zip/Postal Code: _____

*New York residents remit applicable sales taxes.
Canadian residents remit applicable GST and provincial taxes.

◆ HARLEQUIN®

Look us up on-line at: http://www.romance.net

HNFBL4

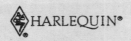

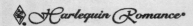

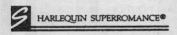

MEN at WORK

All work and no play?
Not these men!

July 1998
MACKENZIE'S LADY by Dallas Schulze

Undercover agent Mackenzie Donahue's
lazy smile and deep blue eyes were his best
weapons. But after rescuing—and kissing!—
damsel in distress Holly Reynolds, how could
he betray her by spying on her brother?

August 1998
MISS LIZ'S PASSION by Sherryl Woods

Todd Lewis could put up a building with ease,
but quailed at the sight of a classroom! Still,
Liz Gentry, his son's teacher, was no battle-ax,
and soon Todd started planning some
extracurricular activities of his own....

September 1998
A CLASSIC ENCOUNTER
by Emilie Richards

Doctor Chris Matthews was intelligent, sexy
and *very* good with his hands—which made
him all the more dangerous to single mom
Lizette St. Hilaire. So how long could she
resist Chris's special brand of TLC?

Available at your favorite retail outlet!

MEN AT WORK™

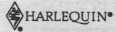 HARLEQUIN®  Silhouette®

Look us up on-line at: http://www.romance.net

PMAW2

HARLEQUIN PRESENTS®

Everyone has special occasions in their life—an engagement, a wedding, an anniversary...or maybe the birth of a baby.

These are times of celebration and excitement, and we're delighted to bring you a special new series called...

One special occasion—that changes your life forever!

Celebrate *The Big Event!* with great books by some of your favorite authors:

September 1998—BRIDE FOR A YEAR
by Kathryn Ross (#1981)
October 1998—MARRIAGE MAKE UP
by Penny Jordan (#1983)
November 1998—RUNAWAY FIANCÉE
by Sally Wentworth (#1992)
December 1998—BABY INCLUDED!
by Mary Lyons (#1997)

Look in the back pages of any *Big Event* book to find out how to receive a set of sparkling wineglasses.

Available wherever Harlequin books are sold.

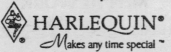

HARLEQUIN®
Makes any time special ™